Addition

Addition

Toni Jordan

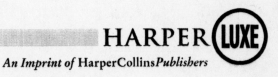

HARPER LUXE

An Imprint of HarperCollins Publishers

This book was originally published in 2008 in Australia by The Text Publishing Company. Published by arrangement with The Text Publishing Company.

FIRST HARPERLUXE EDITION

HarperLuxe™ is a trademark of HarperCollins Publishers

Library of Congress Cataloging-in-Publication Data is available upon request.

ISBN: 978-0-06-176398-4

09 10 11 12 13 ID/RRD 10 9 8 7 6 5 4 3 2 1

To Robert Luke Stanley-Turner
Sanx

Author's Note

This story takes place in my home, a land sometimes called "down under." This land is like yours in many ways, but in other ways it is very different. Our summer months are December, January and February, and our winter, June, July and August. Our temperatures are measured in Celsius; a summer's day of 36 is almost 97 degrees Fahrenheit, and a cooler day of 12 is a more pleasant 54. We measure length in centimeters—one is almost half an inch. We also eat pancakes and drink coffee, and go shopping and to football games (although of a different sort).

Chapter 1

It all counts.

Not long after the accident, I turned at the gate on my way to school one morning and looked back at the front stairs. There were only 10—normal-looking gray concrete, not like the 22 treacherous wooden steps at the back. The front stairs had a small set of lines and some gray sand set in the middle so you wouldn't slip in bad weather. Somehow it seemed wrong to have walked down them unawares. I felt bad about it. Ungrateful to those stairs that had borne my weight uncomplaining for all of my 8 years. I walked back to the stairs and climbed to the top. Then I started down again but this time I counted each one. There. 10.

The day went on but I couldn't stop thinking about those 10 stairs. Not obsessing. Nothing that kept me

from schoolwork or skipping or talking, but a gentle teasing like the way your tongue is drawn to a loose front tooth. On the way home it seemed natural to count my steps from the school gate, down the path, over the footpath, across the road, along the street at the bottom of the hill, across another road, up the hill and then into our yard: 2,827.

A lot of steps for so short a distance, but I was smaller then. I'd like to do that walk again now that I'm 172 centimeters instead of 120, and I might one day. I can only remember lying in bed at the end of that first day, triumphant. I had measured the dimensions of my world, and I knew them, and now no one could change them.

Unlike the weather in Melbourne. 36 degrees and sunny; 38 and the same; 36 and the same; 12 and raining so hard I risk concussion getting the mail. This January has been like that, so far. When I was a kid I could hardly stand it. From the age of 8 I graphed each day's max and min from the newspapers, desperate for a pattern.

In time, counting became the scaffolding of my life. What's the best way to stop nonchalantly, so as not to arouse suspicion should someone interrupt? It's okay to stop, it doesn't break the rules—the numbers are patient and will wait, provided you don't forget where

you are up to or take an extra pace. But whatever you do, don't lose count or you'll have to start again. It's hard to stop the involuntary twitching, though.

"Grace, why are your fingers moving like that?"

"Like what?"

Funny how I sensed this wasn't something to be discussed with other people, even when I was 8.

The numbers were a secret that belonged only to me. Some kids didn't even know the length of the school or their house, much less the number of letters in their own name. I am a 19: Grace Lisa Vandenburg. Jill is a 20: Jill Stella Vandenburg, one more than me despite being three years younger. My mother is a 22: Marjorie Anne Vandenburg. My father was a 19 too: James Clay Vandenburg.

10s began to resonate. Why do things almost always end in zeros? Crossing a road was 30. From the front fence to the shop was 870. Was I subconsciously decimalizing my count? Did I stop at the shop's doormat, rather than the door, so it would end in a zero?

Zeros. 10s. Fingers, toes. The way we name the numbers, in blocks. One day in math we learned rounding, changing a number to the nearest one divisible by 10. I asked Mrs. Doyle the word for moving a number to the nearest divisible by 7. She didn't know what I meant.

Why are clocks so obviously wrong? Counting on a base of 60 is a pagan tendency. Why do people tolerate it?

By the time I finished high school I knew about the digital system and its Hindu-Arabic history and the role of Fibonacci in gaining support for base 10 in 1202. There's still anger out there in cyberspace—flat-earthers upset that base 10 was chosen over base 12, which they consider purer: easy to halve and quarter, the number of the months and of the apostles. But to me it's about the fingers—it's the way the body's been designed. No debate.

Realizing the world was driven by 10s was a beautiful turning point, like someone had given me the key. When tidying my room, I started picking up 10 things. 10 things an hour, 10 things a day. 10 brushes of my hair. 10 grapes from the bunch for a little lunch. 10 pages of my book to read before sleep. 10 peas to eat. 10 socks to fold. 10 minutes to shower. 10. Now I could see not just the dimensions of my world, but the size and shape of everything in it. Defined, clear and in its place.

My Barbie Country Camper was out; my Cuisenaire rods were in. On the outside they don't look like much. Green plastic box; inside, bits of wood, cut and smoothed, in various sizes and colors. Invented

by Georges Cuisenaire, my second-favorite inventor, while he was looking for a way to make math easier for children. I love them, especially the colors. Each rod has a number that corresponds to its length, and each number is a different color. For years into my adult life, numbers were also colors. White was 1. Red was 2. Light green was 3. Pink (a hot, sticky pink) was 4. Yellow was 5. Dark green was 6. Black was 7. Brown was 8. Blue was 9. Orange (although I'd always thought of it as tan, a small vowel shift) was 10.

I spent hours lying on my bed, holding my rods, listening to the tink as they knocked together. When I hear that sound I am 8 years old again: the bed on a diagonal poking from a corner of the room; easier for my mother to tuck in from both sides. The sheets, flannelette with 34 pastel pink and blue stripes that I counted at night instead of sheep. Along the east wall were 4 dormer windows to catch the morning sun, the 31 slats of the aluminum venetians pulled high. The head of the bed had a built-in light behind a translucent plastic screen, and a shelf that held a small transistor radio, untarnished silver in a mock-leather case, a birthday present from my grandfather. There were more shelves on the west wall that held 2 china figurines, a shepherdess and a mermaid, and 3 stuffed Pekingese dogs with long caramel hair that I brushed each night:

father, mother and baby. There was a bride doll in a satin gown garnished with 40 pearls. On the floor in the corner were 7 tin cars the size of a child's fist, left behind after playing.

At school everything was normal. Better than normal. A-plus, A-plus, A-plus. *And top of the class, again, is Grace Vandenburg.* The secret of my success was numbers: each week I did 100 minutes of homework for each subject, and when the work was done I memorized 10 words from the beginning of the dictionary. Aardvark, aback, abacus, abalone, abandon, abase, abashed, abate, abattoirs, abbess, accident. My memory was sharpened and primed with words and numbers—facts and figures, dates and words still stick today, even when I don't intend it.

When I fell in love with numbers, no one noticed. No one would have noticed if I'd been set on fire. That was a bad year for my parents. My mother would spend hours in the garden cradling every seedling as if the death of even one would diminish her. By then, my father had already begun to fade. Jill and I fended for ourselves. Counting became, and remained, my secret.

I live here in Glen Iris, 2 blocks from where I grew up. I live alone, except for Nikola. (Nikola Tesla: 11.) His photo is in a polished silver frame on my bedside table,

right next to my Cuisenaire rods. The picture was taken in 1885 when he was 29 by Napoleon Sarony, the famous photographer—the original hangs in the Smithsonian in Washington, DC, next to an induction motor Nikola invented in 1888. His hair is neatly parted and slicked down, although the right side refuses to lie flat. It's cut short above his ears, which are too large for his delicate head and which lie backward on an angle: a greyhound sensing prey. His mustache is also asymmetrical, certainly presentable enough, not scruffy by any means but not preened either. He is wearing a white shirt with the collar pinned down inside his suit coat, which is darker and striped, with narrow lapels that I assume were usual at the time. But it's his eyes that show the world who he is. Deep set, dark—staring straight ahead. To the future.

I've stared at that photo for 20 years now. I wouldn't be surprised if he spoke one day. If the grayscale melted into warm flesh and his lips started moving. "My name is Nikola Tesla," he'd say. "I was born at midnight between the 9th and 10th of July, 1856, in Croatia. My mother was Djuka Mandic and my father was Milutin Tesla. My brother was Dane and my sisters were Milka, Angelina and Marica. I studied engineering at the Austrian Polytechnic School in Graz. I emigrated to the United States in 1884, where

I discovered electricity, magnetism, the AC motor, robotics, radar and wireless communication. I never married, nor had a girlfriend. My friends included Mark Twain, William K. Vanderbilt and Robert Underwood Johnson. I hate jewelry on women. I love pigeons."

I'll be lying on the bed when I hear this, and I'll roll over to face him. "My name is Grace Lisa Vandenburg," I'll say. "I am 35 years old. My mother, Marjorie Anne, is 70 and my sister, Jill Stella, is 33. Jill is married to Harry Venables; he's 40 on the second of May. They have 3 children: Harry Junior is 11, Hilary is 10 and Bethany is 6. My father's name was James Clay Vandenburg and he died. I am a teacher, although I'm not working now. I was in love when I was 21. He was funny and clever and wanted to be a filmmaker. His name was Chris and he looked a bit like Nick Cave. I lost my virginity in his car outside my mother's house. It took 4 months before I realized he was also sleeping with his flatmate. I don't like coriander. I don't understand interpretive dance. I don't like realist paintings. Lycra makes me look fat."

Scratch that bit. Possibly I wouldn't fill up the head space of the greatest genius the world has ever known with this riveting detail. He would understand, though. He'd understand me. He was also in love with numbers, but he didn't care much for 10s.

The love of numbers takes many forms, although 10s are obviously and anatomically superior. In one famous case, an 18-year-old boy was obsessed with 22. Imagine walking through doorways 22 times. Sitting in a chair, then immediately standing again, 22 times before you could finally rest. It highlights the inherent logic of 10s. There was a 13-year-old girl who had 9s—tapping her feet on the side of her bed 9 times before she could sleep or rise. There are a number of reports of 8s, including a boy who had to spin around 8 times whenever he entered a room. The 6 story is probably the saddest. This teenager loathed the number so much he couldn't repeat anything 6 times. Or 60. Or 66. He even detested numbers that added up to 6. No 42s. No 33s.

Nikola loved 3s. He counted his steps like me, but it was 3s that captured his heart. He would only stay in a hotel room if the number was divisible by 3. Each night when he ate his dinner at the Waldorf-Astoria, at precisely 8:00 P.M. at his usual table, he had 18 napkins folded beside him. Why 18? Why not 6 or 9 or 72? I'd love to roll over in bed one morning, see him next to my pillow and ask him. This year on August 27 I turn 36. He'd love that.

Walking the streets of New York was difficult for him because if he went more than halfway around a city block he needed to keep going until he had walked

around it 3 times. Instead of counting food the way I do, he calculated the cubic volume of each forkful or plateful or glass; he didn't care if he ate two beans or twenty. This kind of mental gymnastics takes some concentration even for the world's greatest genius, so he always ate alone. He loved playing cards, which I've long suspected is a way of channeling a love of counting. Gambling is one of the few things Nikola and I disagree on. Cards and wheels don't behave in any kind of pattern despite the desperate hopes of those sad casino addicts. Back in 1876 Nikola had become a gambler, which worried his father, a minister of religion. But he conquered this vice, like he conquered smoking and drinking coffee, because he could conquer anything.

The front stairs at our house started me counting, but I sometimes imagine how it all began. There are so many possibilities, but it had to start somewhere. With someone. One person.

In my most usual imaginings it's a Cro-Magnon woman. It's not that men weren't capable, but men protected the tribe and hunted—numbers were less important to them. It's the women who needed them more.

A group of women collecting wild grains or fruit or caring for children. They would need to measure things

like when a baby was due or how many days of food were left. More than 10,000 years ago, she would have been on a trip, maybe to visit another tribe, and perhaps she wanted to know when her period would come. The tribe had some rules, say: a menstruating woman couldn't handle food, or mix with men or skin game. She may have needed animal skin torn into strips. She didn't want to be unprepared. It was late winter and the sky was overcast. She couldn't see the moon. She took something extra with her on that journey. She took the radius bone of a wolf that she had found one day while looking for ptarmigan eggs. She picked up that bone without really knowing why but, on the day before her journey and the first day of her period, she marked it with a piece of flint that had broken off a spearhead. She drew a line:

|

Would she have been heralded as a great benefactor, the giver of a way to know how many bison were in a herd or how many days' walk to the ocean? Prized as a mate, a mother, a senior member of the tribe? Perhaps it would have been too different, this way of seeing. Was she ostracized or punished or bullied because her insight was greater? Was she alone, sent away because

she defied the moon and the seasons and the knowledge that they bring?

It started as a row of notches; but it didn't take long for the notches to be grouped in finger-lots of 5. Then the groups of 5 became 4 downward strokes with 1 cross stroke through them. In fact the Arabic numerals 2 and 3 come from those strokes. A 2 is just two horizontal strokes joined together; a 3 is three joined strokes. Eventually special symbols would evolve for 5 and 10, to end the repetition of all those strokes. Yet there's purity in those simple marks, the kind you still see on children's blackboards. We all count with our hearts when we are young. At teachers' college most of my classmates aspired to teach upper secondary, but primary school was all I ever wanted. Seeing small children learn to count thrilled me year after year, as if it were me drawing those marks for the very first time. I remember everything about being a teacher. The feeling of chalk dust, silky against my palms. The wonder and mischief on those little faces.

Sometimes at night, after all the day's counting is done, I imagine I am the woman who finds the numbers first. The woman who cut the marks into the wolf's bone. I am to be sacrificed for my heresy. It is always Nikola who saves me.

Sometimes I'm in Salem, Massachusetts. My Puritan-black smock is laced tight over my breasts. My

wrists are bound behind my back, around a stake piled with branches for burning. From waist to ankles my legs have been pressed together and tied by my church-going neighbors, who take the chance to force rough-ened hands under my skirts, lingering over my calves, my thighs. The crowd jeers. The fire is lit. There is no hope for me. I am to be devoured by the flames. Suddenly, the crowd falls silent. A black horse thun-ders through the night. It is Nikola. He walks toward me, the flames curling around his knee-length black boots. He is unburned. Unharmed. He snaps my ties and cradles me against his chest.

Other times my wrists are bound in front of me and I am kneeling before the Aztec high priest. My eyes and mouth are open wide. My clothing, elaborate gilded and jeweled cloth wound around my body, is removed by two guards who stand on either side, hands on my shoulders. They tie a silken blindfold over my eyes. One guard cups my naked breast insolently. I am helpless. They haul me to my feet by a chain around my throat and bend me over an altar. A cold hand presses against the nape of my neck. Abruptly I sense a change in the crowd—murmurs, scuffling. I am hauled from the altar, lifted over Nikola's shoulder. My blindfold falls to the ground. The guards lie dead, the high priest groveling.

It's a teenage fairy-tale fantasy, I know, but so vivid sometimes that real life seems pale. At least it's not

like the typical middle-class fantasies of a middle-class woman from a middle-class suburb. I can imagine how they go: "Take me on the granite countertop, Julio! Let me see your pumping arse reflected in the European double-door stainless steel fridge with ice maker!"

In my fantasies, I am always about to die and Nikola always saves me. I have never been to Europe or America or Asia, but my fantasies show me exotic places I can smell and touch and feel. My dreams have no numbers in them, none at all; no counting, no signage, no paces. I wake, and count again.

It's Saturday. It is 24 degrees, an annoying number because technically "room temperature" is between 20 and 23 degrees. I wake at 5:55 A.M. I have 5 minutes to gather myself, then my feet hit the floor the second the numbers roll around to 6:00. (I check the time on the Internet at 6:00 P.M. every night and readjust all my clocks and my watch if necessary. It is rarely necessary.) The rest of Glen Iris might have morphed overnight from leafy streetscape to alien-inhabited moonscape. I never open the blinds.

I stand. 25 paces to the bathroom. Luckily my legs are long for my height. If I had to face a 27 or a 28 so early in the morning it would throw out my day. Brush my teeth—this is tricky. Each tooth has 3 surfaces—

inner, top and outer, except for the front row, which has only 2 surfaces because the tops are sharpened like a razor blade. There are 6 rows—top left, center, top right, bottom left, center, bottom right. Each surface needs 10 full strokes of the brush, back and forth. This means 16 times 10 strokes. 160. It takes a little while. Then floss up and down between each tooth 10 times.

Shower. When scrubbing each limb 10 times with soap it's important not to be heavy handed. Hair: washed every second day and counted out in the circles formed by each finger pressing against my scalp. 10 circles for each finger, and move to another place on my head. Repeat 10 times. The conditioner needs less— only 10 times 5. Out of the shower, dry myself with a towel from the top of the pile. Again, 10 wipes on each limb, 10 for the chest and 10 for the back. Wash my face. My face is divided into 5 zones: forehead—pale, wide, smooth. Each cheek, defined by sharp cheekbones. One nose, a little too pointy. And one chin, prominent. The overall effect is attractive but sharp, like a Scandinavian maître d' wearing underpants a size too small. Each zone needs 5 wipes with a cotton pad to remove the cleanser. Repeat with toner. Use the same action to apply moisturizer. Repeat with sunscreen. Dry hair, 100 slow strokes with the big brush under the dryer. This is the most difficult part because

each stroke must be full and complete right to the tips down the small of my back, yet gentle so I don't end up with a halo of blonde frizz. The only variation to this is Sunday morning, when I also trim my nails and push back the cuticles and cut them, and buff the nails 10 times each with each side of my buffer. There are 4 sides to my buffer: a file, a ridge remover, a smoother and a polisher. This, too, takes a while.

But it isn't Sunday. Back to the bedroom, another 25 steps. I have 10 pairs of knickers and 5 bras. These are folded in the appropriate drawers and I select from the top. Each bra I wear 5 times and each pair of knickers once. I have 10 pairs of trousers and 10 skirts. I have 10 short-sleeved tops and 10 long-sleeved tops. The trousers and long-sleeved tops are, of course, for the cold months and I wear them alternating on a daily basis from April 15, which is halfway through autumn, until October 15, halfway through spring. For the actual winter months of June, July and August I add a jacket regardless of the temperature. The skirts and short-sleeved shirts are for the other half of the year. Each top is worn once and each pair of trousers or skirt 5 times if its first day is a Monday, but only twice if its first day is a Saturday.

I start at the left of my wardrobe and work toward the right, because after I have washed and ironed my

clothes I hang them back at the right side. The order is random, determined by how I hang them on the line, which is determined by the order in which I remove them from the washing machine; I put my hand in and pull out the first piece of cloth I touch. I don't worry about coordination but there is a disproportionate amount of solid, dark color in my wardrobe. Patterns and prints are asking for trouble. I have 10 pairs of shoes: day and evening shoes for each half of the year, plus boots, sneakers, Ugg boots, slippers, old sneakers and a pair of sandals that don't fit but make up the 10. The evening shoes don't get much wear because I haven't been out in the evening for a while.

So now I'm ready for breakfast. It's 7:45.

As it's Saturday, after breakfast I go to the supermarket. At 8:45 on Saturday morning in January in Glen Iris the supermarket is deserted—everyone is still asleep in their beach houses at Portsea or Anglesea or Phillip Island, dreaming about whomever it is they dream about while they lay beside their spouses. Waiting for me at the checkout is a handsome boy, twenty-something, with too much enthusiasm on his pink face. Either he's still full of love for all mankind from last night's ecstasy or he's waiting for the right time to talk to me about Amway. Still, there's no other checkout open. The boy smiles encouragingly. I feel a headache

coming on. I push my shopping trolley over, squeaking with each step.

My trolley has 2 trays of chicken thighs, fat and glossy, each tray containing 5; a carton of eggs marked as a dozen (each week I assure ecstasy boy or high-pain-threshold girl, a Kiwi backpacker with seven piercings in each ear, that I have already checked the eggs. This is so they won't open the carton and notice I have removed 2 and left them in the assorted spices); plastic bags containing 100 beans (that's a pain), 10 carrots, 10 baby potatoes, 10 small onions; 100 grams of salad mix (I refuse to shop in a supermarket without a digital scale); 10 little tins of tuna; 10 orange bottles of shampoo; 9 bananas.

What?

Count again.

How the fuck did I get 9 bananas in my trolley?

This is impossible. I look behind the eggs, behind the bag of beans. This is not possible.

The drug-addled multilevel marketer is standing behind the counter, smiling. Those teeth are money well spent. He's got a smile like a Scientologist's. Well, I'm going back. I can't buy 9 bananas. He can wait while I go back to aisle 12 and get another.

Just as I am about to excuse myself, someone comes to a stop behind me with a basket hanging over his

arm; now I'll lose my spot. And I was here first. What kind of a Nigel No-friends is at the supermarket this early on a Saturday anyway? Must have had a big Friday night with *Inspector Morse* on DVD and a cup of hot cocoa. The Scientologist drug dealer is still standing there. His smile is fading. He folds his arms.

The guy with the basket is reading *Celebrity Nose Jobs,* or some other Pulitzer-winning publication picked from the display near the checkout. He must be nearsighted because he's holding the magazine about one inch from his face. All I can see is his forearms below shirtsleeves scrunched up to his elbows. His forearms are smooth on the underside. One has a tendon taut from the weight of the basket. Dark blond hair on the front. Not too much. Not extending to the back of the square, capable hands. Dangling over the edge of his basket amid 2 trays of mince, 3 trays of sausages, a jar of chili paste and 3 apples is 1 unfettered banana.

The key to an operation like this is nonchalance. I smile, piranha-like, at the Scientologist. He fiddles with his tie. I start loading my groceries onto the belt at the end farthest from the scanner. All except the bananas. The belt rolls onward, remorselessly. It could care less about the bananas.

"I'm exhausted," I say.

He jumps. Whoever trained him should have mentioned that customers sometimes speak.

"I spent all day yesterday collecting spare change for the Red Cross. Famine relief. For the kiddies." I wink. His smile returns. I beckon him closer with a crooked finger and wave my hand over the groceries. I lower my voice to just above a whisper. "Do you mind if I pay for this lot in 5-cent pieces?"

His eyes bug and as he says "I have to check with the manager," his voice breaks. He spins around looking for somebody, anybody. While he's distracted I nonchalantly pick up the bananas from my trolley with both hands. Nonchalantly I rock back, then ever so nonchalantly I spin around, reach my arms full stretch, grab the shriveled brown end of Nigel's banana and lift it out of his basket. He can't see a thing from behind that magazine.

By the time my prospective money-laundering cultist has looked back, all he sees is me smiling eerily, hands up like I'm about to crown Miss Universe with a bunch of bananas. A bunch of 10 bananas that I lay gently on the belt.

"Never mind about the coins," I say, pulling a fifty from my purse. "Not everyone's a cheapskate."

Operation Restore Banana is complete. My groceries are bagged and paid for. I stop for a minute or two

to scan the headlines of the pile of newspapers near the door. Humming the theme to *The Great Escape,* I walk out of the store, 2 bags in each hand. In the parking lot I lean over for a moment to readjust the plastic bags before they amputate my fingers. I straighten. Someone is standing right in front of me.

It's Nigel No-friends. In his right hand is an apple. He throws the apple in the air and catches it.

Chapter 2

"Yes?" You learn imperiousness at teachers' college.

"I wondered if you'd like an apple." He smiles like we're friends, and one eyebrow raises. Nice white teeth. Brown eyes with crinkles around them. 12 around one eye, 14 the other. On top of his head perches a pair of Wayfarers, circa 1986. He works outdoors, I'd say; thinnish build but his biceps and forearms are defined. His shirt is red with some kind of logo. Smooth tan skin. Faded blue jeans. He's 10, maybe 11 centimeters taller than I am. The small waves in his blond hair look damp, like he raced to the supermarket after getting out of the shower. Or perhaps he's been sweating. Occasionally his nostrils flare.

I don't answer. I put the bags down and fold my arms.

"It's a nice apple. Crispy. You could take this apple, and give me back my banana." He holds the apple out.

" 'My banana'? Did you say 'My banana'?"

He nods. He's biting his bottom lip.

"Had you paid for it?"

He laughs, head tilting back. "Not exactly. But it was in my basket."

"That 'my' thing again." I roll my eyes and speak slowly. "It was the supermarket's banana, because you hadn't paid for it. And now it's mine, because I have. It was also the supermarket's basket. It was your . . . nothing."

"Well, this is my apple, because I have paid for it." He pretends to throw it up again, but instead hands it to me. "A small gift for your kind explanation of property law."

The apple is smooth in my hand, and warm from where his hand has been. "That's nothing. I can also explain microeconomic reform using two baguettes, an empty toilet paper roll and a mousetrap." I rest the apple on top of the shampoo. I pick up the bags and start to walk off. He starts walking with me. Like we're walking together.

"And all that shampoo? What does that explain— the stock exchange? Are you cornering the market?" Hands, sans apple, are thrust in the back pockets of his jeans. His tight jeans.

I stop again. "Are you doing a survey?"

"Just curious. You have vegetables and fruit and chicken probably for one week for one person. But shampoo for more. It makes me wonder."

"Supermodels. Me and 29 other supermodels live in a big house together, painting each other's toenails and having pillow fights in our pajamas. So this is food and shampoo for one week."

He leans a long arm into my left-hand bag and uncovers the potatoes.

"Don't think I'm doubting you. You could be a supermodel. But I'm pretty sure that supermodels don't eat potatoes. Also you don't have any celery. Or sprouts. Or Perrier."

"You're right. I'm kidding about the supermodels. Actually I'm stockpiling shampoo. The horsemen of the apocalypse are nigh."

He shakes his head and frowns, momentarily saddened by the thought of the end of the world. He looks down at my bags again like the contents might have changed in the last 10 seconds. "No water, though? Is this some kind of magic dry shampoo? Anyway, the horsemen won't care what you look like."

"No water will be necessary, because the horsemen will be swimming in on rising sea levels. And they will care what I look like. I think the Bible says some-

thing about the meek and the blow-dried inheriting the earth."

We say nothing for one millisecond longer than is comfortable.

"Thanks for the apple. Next time I eat fruit salad I'll think of you." I walk across the parking lot. I don't look back.

I used to be good at flirting. A lot of people think that flirting's about sex. Well, flirting's about surprise, and surprise is about sex. If someone can be unexpected using words, imagine how thrilling they could be using their mouth. Or their tongue. Or their teeth.

I'm good at flirting because lots of conversations run through my head all the time with lots of different outcomes. I've always been good at taking people by surprise. In fact the more nervous I become the more sentences and thoughts and numbers fly around my brain, looking for but not finding a way out. Take one comment that someone makes, and think of all the possible replies. How many replies would be logical? Well, if the comment is "What color is the sky today?"—the reply would be limited to, say, 15 or 16 choices. But if someone says "And all that shampoo? What does that explain?" there could be 100, maybe 200, appropriate replies. And if each reply invites 200 other remarks already we have 40,000 possibilities in 3

sentences. And some conversations have 50 sentences, so it's impossible to plan ahead. The trick is to say the first thing that pops into your head.

Back when I was teaching, after school on a Friday some of us would go to the pub up the road for drinks. One night, not long before it ended, we had all had a few and I was sitting at the bar chatting to a lovely man called Gav. All right, flirting. He was a bricklayer and he wore heavy boots dusted with cement, black jeans and a blue striped shirt. He had a nice smile. One of the other teachers was pissed. He came up behind Gav and whispered in his ear, but I could hear it clearly, even over the music. Don't waste your time, mate. She might look hot but she's a fucking nutcase.

I leave the apple on a fence halfway down the next street.

Tonight I dream of Nikola, except he has blond hair with small damp waves. After he saves me, after he kisses me, he puts his hand on the curve of my belly, his big hand spread flat. He slips his fingers under the band of my skirt. I can feel his breath in my ear. His hand reaches down my pants and he presses against my clitoris, sudden and steady and hard with his thumb rough from his experiments. I gasp. When I wake I lie very still. I can still feel it.

At **Melbourne** international airport there is no gate 13. The gates go up to 11 in odd numbers and to 14 in even numbers. They say I'm the fucking nutcase but everyone has it. The fear of 13 is deep inside people, in that part of them that's more animal than human. Imagine the announcement: "Attention, please. Flight number 911 to New York City is now boarding at gate 13." How many people would get on that plane? Rational people. Educated people. The fear of the number 13 is called triskaidekaphobia. Almost everyone has it. They work, they have friends, partners. No one tries to make them take drugs.

When I was teaching I always talked about fears. Kids love that stuff. They loved conquering long, tongue-twister words as much as I loved teaching them. I remember their favorites: ablutophobia, the fear of bathing; ailurophobia, the fear of cats; and of course, arachibutyrophobia, the fear of peanut butter sticking to the roof of your mouth.

As usual, I received complaints from the parents. *How will this improve Bilynda's scores at high school?* As usual, I couldn't tell them the truth about their children's lives, their own lives. That they are color-blind. They are tone-deaf. They are ants racing across my balcony as the sun is rising only to race back as it sets.

They will get jobs in offices and most will work well enough for their feed. They will meet another ant of the same or opposite sex and will borrow more money than their grandparents could imagine and use their freedom as collateral to buy a double-fronted weatherboard between a park and a train station. If they breed they will make more worker ants to guarantee economic growth and more taxpayers to pay for more politicians and poorer-quality schools. When they retire they will receive not a gold watch but an indexed pension. Their children ants will move away to be spared their parents' grasping, wallowing lack of productivity. The parents will spend their miserable pension on pills—for their arthritis, diabetes and heart disease, and the four-sided blue one so they can still get stiff or wet to remind them of when, for 4 minutes twice a week, their rutting made them feel alive. For their last few years they will live in a garbage dump filled with other refuse ants and they will stare at the walls and the ceiling till they know each crack and chip as well as they once knew their own ant face. They will die painlessly due to the advances of modern drug therapy, as numb and vapid as they lived. Their belongings will scatter and they will cease.

I never told the parents this.

Now I live on a sickness benefit. I'm incapacitated, everyone says, and I can't work anymore. So instead of

going to school each day at exactly 8:00 to supervise the
playground I stay home in my flat in Glen Iris. Typi-
cal sixties pale brick 6-pack. Ugly. My neighbors are a
doddering dementiac, a thirtysomething permanently
attached to her mobile phone, a coterie of Asian students
whose cooking can be smelled in the next suburb, and
two dreary couples—one pair androgynously similar à
la David Bowie 1976, and the other frighteningly dif-
ferent, perhaps a Hells Angel and a librarian.

My flat is on the top floor. I have a bedroom, small
and crowded, with just my single bed and a chest of
drawers. The cupboards are built in. I have a bath-
room, an airy kitchen where I eat, and a living room
with cream walls and dark green carpet and all my
books. My books are mostly encyclopedias and refer-
ence, although I occasionally fool around with fiction—
Umberto Eco, Camus, Conan Doyle. I have a bookcase
with 5 shelves and each shelf has 30 books. On some
shelves, 30 is a real squeeze—the books are tucked in,
buried next to their sisters until they cannot breathe.
On other shelves 30 is spacious and there is room for a
knickknack from my childhood: a snow dome that says
"Greetings from the Gold Coast" or a peeling frame
holding my parents' yellow wedding photo. My parents
have smiling faces from another age, smiling because
they can't yet know their future. Stop smiling! Run!

The books are in alphabetical order, by title; *Gray's Anatomy* snuggles next to *Great Moments in Mathematics*. *Biography Today: Scientists and Inventors* caresses *A Brief History of Disease, Science and Medicine*. In years past I have sectioned them by topic: science, medicine, mathematics. But now they are all together, mingling and flirting.

I have a small balcony. Staying home all day gives me more time for serious counting. I still do some tutoring; 5 kids, cash in hand. Math. The parents know all about me, that I make each child sit in my small kitchen and do each exercise in his book 5 times and that I don't let the kids advance until every exercise is done. One of the mothers came to the first 2 sessions to make sure I wasn't going to drop Toby from my second-story window. I can imagine her reporting back to the others. "She's mad, that's for sure, and she couldn't look after a whole room full of children. But she makes him do all the examples and even if he gets it wrong she explains it in a quiet voice and makes him do it again. She never loses her patience like the other teachers do. She just sits there and watches him do his sums over and over." I can imagine what the parents say. What everyone says. She can't work, can't travel. She has no proper social life. I'm sure they could come up with numbered lists of the things I can't do. And life would be different if I didn't count, I know that.

But without it the world would be too big and too changeable. An endless void. I'd be lost all the time. I'd be overwhelmed.

Another busy week has flown by, filled with counting. Went to the café. Did housework. Spoke to my niece on the phone. Received a new book, *Handbook of Functional Gastrointestinal Disorders*, in the mail and read it. Twice. Had a weird craving for apple juice, which I don't buy because it's not on my shopping list. I don't even like apples.

It's Friday. 13 degrees. It's exactly 10:30 A.M. I leave the house on foot, like I do every day. 150 steps to the corner, then 400 to the next corner. 20 to cross the street. 325 to the next corner, then 25 paces to the front of the café. At exactly 10:48 A.M. I reach the café. The café is right across the road from the park. It's a nondescript kind of place with wicker chairs and glass-topped tables. It screams Parisian. On the wall are Monets, the same prints you see in every frame shop on Main Street. At the back is a grainy laminate counter with a cash register, a cake stand holding 11 banana muffins stacked in 3 layers and a candy-striped bowl for tips. I'd like to know how much is there but from the door I can't count it.

This is how it happens: I will walk in. I will take the first available table, starting from the top left-hand

corner and proceeding around the room and inward in a clockwise direction. I sit. Cheryl will see me from wherever she stands—behind the counter or clearing another table or delivering an order. She is tall and about 50. (I'm working on a plan to find out, because it's annoying not knowing how old exactly. I'm considering asking her "What moisturizer do you use, because your skin looks so great for your age?" Then she'll ask me "How old do you think I am?" Then I'll say "About 40?" Then she'll laugh and say "I'm actually 48!") She has long dark hair worn loose swinging down her back. Not very hygienic for someone in food services. She has a smile she rations, with a tiny hint of gold filling peeking out on a left upper molar. She wears a black apron around her waist and a pen behind her ear. Then she speaks: a random choice between "Nice day, eh, love?" and "Shocking weather." It'd be nice if she could oscillate between these or even choose specific clichés for each day of the week, but that's the trouble with small business. No systems.

Cheryl will say "What'll you have, love?" as if there's a question, as if there's any doubt in my mind or hers. If we lived in New York I'm sure she'd say "Usual, pal?" but she never acknowledges that there is a usual. Perhaps she has a bet with her friends waiting for the day I order something else.

But I never order something else. I order a hot chocolate with 2 marshmallows and a slice of orange cake. While she's gone I double-check the tables. 17. The chairs. 59. 1 missing. Perhaps it's in the kitchen so tired cooks can rest their feet. It takes between 3 and 7 minutes for Cheryl to bring my order, depending on the number of people in the café, and she says, "Here you go, love. You enjoy that."

I do enjoy it. I dunk my 2 marshmallows in the hot chocolate and stir, and its layers swirl into consistency. It is hot and sweet with foam on the top like a cappuccino. The cake is my favorite part of the whole day. It is a flourless orange cake, moist and crumbly, with pieces of softened orange peel spread evenly through. It has a cream-cheese icing and is sprinkled, not coated but sprinkled, with poppy seeds. And the chef is not consistent—some days there are 12 tiny seeds spread out like anthills in the desert. Other times there are 50 huddled as if there's a stiff wind, or there are 75 squished on the small piece of cake like flattened children on the train coming home from the fair.

First, I count them.

Then this number, the number of seeds, is the number of bites I must take to eat the piece of cake.

Anywhere between 20 and 30 is no hardship—I generally take small bites while I sit here drinking my

chocolate. Fewer than 20 needs some skill—mentally divide the piece, calculate how big each forkful must be, then eat it. More than 30 is a large number of bites, and once there was an incredible 92 poppy seeds and I virtually had to eat the cake crumb by crumb.

That's how it's supposed to go, but today when I walk into the café at 10:48 A.M., there are no spare tables. Full. Every one of them full.

No spare tables.

What do I do now? How do I leave? How do I get home?

No table. No table. No table.

There's always a table.

No table. No table. No table.

Then I begin to hear a noise. I listen closely. It is the noise of my blood running through the small capillaries in my ears. It's starting. It's starting again.

I breathe quicker but I'm not getting enough air. My shoulders ache because my joints have unhinged and my arms hang, connected to my body only by the skin. My head spins, praying for an empty table. If I can't sit I can't order my cake and chocolate and if I don't order my cake I won't be able to count the poppy seeds and know how many bites to take and if I don't eat my cake I won't finish my cake and then how will I know when to go home? I'm loose now, there's nothing to bring me back home. I'm loose and the wind blows through me

and I could end up anywhere. I begin to feel cramps in my abdomen. Perhaps this is cholera. Soon all that is in me will leak out.

That's when I see him, the man from the supermarket. He is sitting at the second table from the back on the right-hand wall. He sees me. There is an empty seat at his table. He waves like he's in grade 3.

I wear a watch on my left wrist. It's an old watch, a boy's watch. It should have been my brother's. Everybody has those times when it all becomes a bit overwhelming. When everything becomes too much, I look at my watch. I love its Roman numerals. Love the look of them, as if they are Roman buildings with all those I's like columns of a ruin. Roman numerals are very rarely used now, except for things like the date a movie is made so we don't realize how old it is. Or to number items in a series, like boats or sons or *Rockys*.

There are two things I like best about Roman numerals—first, it's not just the symbols that matter, it's where they are placed. I and V together should equal 6. But if you put the I right before the V, it's 4. XL is 40, CM is 900. Also I like that there are no zeros. The Romans hadn't invented them. That was up to the Hindus.

Sometimes I'd like to crawl inside the face of my brother's watch. I'd walk around the numerals. Touch

them. Balance on the hands. How long can I stand here thinking about numbers?

What is the proper length of time to stand in a café and consider a watch?

The mystery of Roman numerals is this—why do clock (and watch) faces have IIII instead of IV? Surely the Romans knew how to count in their own language? Even Big Ben has IIII instead of IV. The most common answer is that the IIII balances the VIII on the opposite side of the clock face. But I and XI don't balance and no one worries about them. No, the most likely answer is that—despite our evolving strict rules for counting, to control the way the numbers are used, to make them conform—the Romans didn't think that way. Probably IIII was okay because everyone knew it meant 4 and it wasn't such a big deal. They had more to worry about, like getting good seats for the Colosseum and making sure their togas didn't fall off. But maybe the whole IIII/IV business is the real reason the Roman Empire fell. Plenty of empires survive cross-border incursions. There's no recovering from sloppiness.

Whatever the correct amount of time is for standing in a café looking at your watch, it's passed.

Now I have to decide.

Chapter 3

I can wait for the panic to rise until I can't breathe or I can walk over and sit down. If I do that, Cheryl can come over and say something about the weather and bring me my chocolate and my cake and then I can count the seeds and eat the cake and then I can go home. But if I sit there I have to talk to him. That would be 2 conversations with one stranger. Unprecedented.

I go over. 12 paces to the table.

I pull out the chair.

I sit down.

He's got sweet teeth, like the milk teeth of a child. At least the 6 I can see are like that. Creamy white with curves instead of corners and points. He's wearing jeans again today, on a Friday. Great. Not only does he have no friends but he's also unemployed. Still, he

looks good in jeans. He's wearing a black waffle-weave short-sleeved shirt with 6 buttons up the front. The buttons are small and glassy—plastic pretending to be mother-of-pearl. His blond hair is messy. He's offered me his table. I really should be gracious.

"Are you stalking me?" I say.

He's mid-sip of his coffee, and snorts. "Um . . . no. Are you stalking me?"

"Why on earth would I want to stalk you?"

"I don't know . . . to steal my fruit?"

"It was one banana. I've moved on."

"So have I. Really. It's . . . nice to see you again." He picks up the menu. He puts it down again. It sounds as if his brain is leaking.

I check my sarcasm detector. Nothing. Perhaps he means *It's nice to see you again.* Astonishingly, I start to blush. Not a delicate Austenesque two-dusky-pink-circles-in-the-middle-of-my-rounded-girlish-cheeks type blush. More like a swell when you are standing in the ocean, a rolling swell of heat and redness that starts in my toes, thunders up my legs and tickles my labia before finally crashing on the beach of my face. A violent pulsing red.

"That's because you've seen me walking toward you. I'm great at walking. The secret is"—I lean in, peering from side to side conspiratorially, my hand against my

face to stymie eavesdroppers—"one foot in front of the other. My parents taught me many years ago and now I practice almost every day. It's my pet event: walk across café."

He opens his mouth to reply but Cheryl appears at my shoulder. "What'll you have, love?"

Finally.

"1 hot chocolate with 2 marshmallows and a piece of orange cake, please."

"No orange cake today, love. How about a nice piece of lemon tart?"

Fuck.

Fuck.

Don't panic, don't panic, don't panic.

No orange cake means no poppy seeds. No poppy seeds means no predetermined number of bites. How can I eat something with no predetermined number of bites?

I look at Banana Man. "How old are you?"

He doesn't even have the grace to look surprised. People should look taken aback when strangers ask them how old they are while ordering food in a café.

"38."

I turn to Cheryl. "Yes, I'll have the lemon tart."

Cheryl grins. Not at me. "Anything else for you, Shamie? Running late today, are we?"

Shamie. I've been coming here every day for 2 years and I'm just "love."

"Slept in. I had a late one last night. And yes, another coffee, thanks, Cheryl."

Cheryl gives him her juiciest smile. I've never had a smile like that, even on my birthday when I tipped her 10 bucks. Suddenly I hate her. It's her fault I'm sitting at someone else's table and I can't have what I always have. It's her fault I'm surrounded by grinning idiots. She goes to get my orange cake. Playing the role of orange cake today will be lemon tart.

"Running late today? What, she times you?"

He laughs despite the fact it wasn't funny. "I usually run around the park first thing in the morning. Then drop in for a coffee."

Something tells me it's going to take Cheryl longer than 7 minutes to bring my cake today. At least it's going to seem longer. I persevere. "What kind of a name is Shamie anyway?"

"Seamus Joseph O'Reilly. You'll never guess where Mum and Dad came from."

19. Like me. "India?"

"Aah . . . no. If they were from India my name would be Seamus Joseph O'Singh."

Now that we are closer I can see his eyes aren't brown after all. They're hazel.

"Now your turn," he says.

"My turn to do what?"

"This is how people meet and become friends. I say my name, then you say yours. Then we shake hands."

"Really? This is a quaint ritual. Are you an anthropologist?"

My orange cake arrives. It looks suspiciously like lemon tart but I can ignore that. Much harder will be eating it in 38 bites. I've chosen a difficult task here. It's a shame he isn't 14.

Lemon tart is much flatter than orange cake. I would say it has only one third the height. I could easily manage 38 bites with a slice of orange cake but lemon tart will be difficult.

I start by dividing the slice lengthwise down the middle from the point to the crust. Then crosswise, but not bisected exactly because the part near the crust is much wider. More like one third at the crust end and two thirds at the pointy end. The 2 pieces that I now have at the pointy end I divide lengthwise again, then each of these I divide into 3. This gives me 12 pieces at the pointy end. Now for the crust end. I need 26 here, which won't be easy.

I divide each of the 2 pieces at the crust end lengthwise into 3. So far so good. 6. I divide each one of these into 4, crosswise. 24. Then I peel the short crust pastry

away from the filling of the 2 top corners on the outside of the slice. Eureka. 38. I eat piece number 1.

The whole time he's watching me. His eyelashes are inordinately long.

"No, I'm not an anthropologist. Are you a surgeon?" He's still smiling. The dent in his lower lip is gone. His eyebrows are raised.

"Grace. Grace Vandenburg. At the moment I'm resting between assignments and considering my career options. With assistance from the generous taxpayer." Up to piece 6 now.

"I work at the Kino. In the box office."

Whoa. Behind the counter. In a cinema. 2 large popcorns, please. "That sounds exciting."

"I don't mind it. I love movies."

"Not working today?" Piece 12. Luckily there's little chewing involved, because they're such small pieces.

"Day off. I'm going to the tennis match this afternoon. Men's semis." He takes another sip of his coffee. He really has the nicest arms. "You must be pretty hungry."

Piece 14. I gesture to the tart. "Starving. I'm on an all-lemon diet."

A herd of mothers pushing prams comes in. There's a huge pram-centered disruption, chairs and tables being moved. Down to my last 2 pieces now.

I stand up. The tart is finished. The chocolate is only half drunk but I can leave it. The chocolate isn't actually part of it.

"Okay, well thanks for the seat." I put my 9 dollars and 40 cents on the table. Exact change. "I might see you around."

He stands. I'm 2 steps away when he speaks. "When?"

I turn to face him. He's standing next to me. I can see his neck. The shadow under his chin. The beginnings of a wrinkle in front of his ear. I refuse to step back. "What?"

"When might you see me around? I can't predict when you'll next need a banana or a seat. So I'm not sure when I'll see you again."

This makes me smile, I can't help it. God knows I don't want to encourage him, but I can smell his breath and it's warm and faintly musky and it's been inside his body. I can't speak for a moment.

"Look, Grace, I know you don't know me. And I don't know you. But there's a great Italian place up on High Street. We could have dinner. Tomorrow night."

I deliver my sternest look. He continues. "Only it doesn't have to be dinner. It could be just drinks. Or dessert. Or I could have dessert." He tilts his head to catch my eye. "You could have a piece of fruit."

I have stepped into a parallel universe. Things like this do not happen to me. "Are you asking me out?"

"Sometimes I amaze myself. Look, I don't make a habit of asking out women I've only just met, but yes. I am."

"You can't be serious. Some people find me a little . . . abrupt."

"I put that down to the all-lemon diet."

I wipe the smile as soon as I can. "Are you implying I'd be free tomorrow night with such little notice?"

"Sunday night?"

"Busy. Teleconference."

"Monday night?"

"Finishing *Ulysses*."

"Tuesday?"

"Washing my hair."

"Grace Vandenburg, I love a challenge but this is ridiculous."

I sigh. Best get it over with.

"I tend to cut my food into little pieces."

"I noticed."

"This means I'm not always scintillating dinner company."

"Well, I see it this way. I think you've got a lot going on in your head. That's not true of most people I meet. Here . . ." He takes a few steps to the counter, where

there is a pen lying next to the credit card machine. Back at the table, he scrawls on a paper napkin. "This is my mobile number. Friday night then. Say yes. You can always call if you change your mind."

He hands me the napkin. So in my hand, right now, is his number. I glance down—I can see a 2—then I quickly fold the napkin over and look away. He smiles at me with those pretty hazel eyes.

Generally I don't surprise myself. Generally I know myself pretty well. I have my rules and I stick to them. Who knows what could happen if I start making arbitrary decisions and upset the synchronized pattern of the universe?

"Yes," I say.

On the walk home from the café not only do I count but I also fill myself with other thoughts so there is no room left, none at all. I don't think Nikola ever had a date. Apparently he was fond of Anne Morgan, the daughter of the industrialist J. Pierpont, even though she grew into a fat ugly militant feminist. Nikola wasn't the type to marry for money, but considering the way things turned out, that would have got him out of trouble later.

Lots of beautiful and talented women had him in their sights. Sarah Bernhardt. Nellie Melba.

Who wouldn't? A towering 6 feet 6 inches—198 centimeters—with large hands. Piercing blue eyes, staggeringly handsome face. Electric, pardon the pun. There were the usual rumors that he was gay but I don't believe it. Not for a minute. It's just that he had a number of, well, quirks.

He hated jewelry. Pearls especially would make him recoil and he couldn't be in the same room with them. Neo-Freudians take this as proof of his abhorrence of women because pearls represent breasts. I don't buy it. Sometimes a pearl is only a pearl. He didn't hate women. He believed that society would collapse as soon as women became educated. He wasn't one of those men who think we don't have the brains for it. He often spoke about the genius of his mother, Djuka, who ran the farm and the home and was famous in the village for her invention of a better kind of loom. His photographic memory came from her and he felt the waste of her, this country mother of 5 who had never been to school but could recite entire books of Serbian poetry.

Nikola knew that when we became educated like men and joined the workforce we wouldn't be interested in families or babies. As he wasn't. So there's none of his genes left now, because he had no children. Like there'll be none of me left when I die.

The air is heavy and hot. I try to imagine how many people have walked this way, ever. This is a number you could never know, because it goes right back before this century, and before the last. It goes back tens of thousands of years. So many people. Uncountable.

Don't think about it. What kind of name is Seamus, anyway? It's like a joke name. And he works at the cinema, for God's sake. He's a pathetic movie nerd, one of those gormless idiots who wear white short-sleeved shirts carefully ironed by their mother (with whom he undoubtedly still lives) with a super-silky non-silk tie with cartoon characters on it. Probably recites the entire script of *The Blues Brothers.* Orange whip? Orange whip? 3 orange whips. Probably owns an English/ Klingon dictionary. Don't think about him, and do not think about the napkin, folded inside my purse, numbers etched by his hand.

Instead think about how many feet have been here. Think about the air. How often has this heavy air been through other people's lungs? If elements are neither created nor destroyed they must be recycled. This air has been sucked into wet membranous cavities, young and pink, black and cancerous, held for an instant to effect the exchange then blown out again through noses of all shapes, colors, sizes. Threaded through hair and snot, waiting for me to breathe in.

Focus on each breath. Each thought. Categorize. File. He asked me out. I've been on dates before. Not for a while, but I used to have lots of dates. I can remember . . . 5. Anyway I can always cancel. Or not show up. He doesn't have my number or know where I live. I never have to see him again. Of all the sad rituals in this inconsequential life, dating must be the saddest of all. Oh, we have so many things in common. We both eat, shit and have a fear of commitment. Our parents used to yell/ignore/smother us. All this just to get laid. I'd respect him more if he'd been honest and said he wanted to screw me right there in the coffee shop. If he'd stood close to me and lifted up my skirt and grabbed my bottom and shoved me onto the table. If he'd pushed me down so I could feel the table cold against my back and ripped my undies with his hard fingers there and then, letting the cup with my chocolate smash against the ground and . . .

Categorize.

File.

I might go on this date after all.

Chapter 4

Tonight I focus on making dinner. Making dinner is a beautiful example of the world falling into order. I begin at 6:05 P.M., immediately after checking the time. Tonight it's chicken and vegetables, being a Friday. Actually every night is chicken and vegetables. At 5 o'clock I marinate the 2 chicken thighs in the juice of half an orange, one clove of garlic (finely chopped), 10 milliliters of olive oil and 10 black olives. At 6:05 P.M. I put the chicken in a tray (presentation-side down) and slide it under the preheated-before-I-checked-the-clocks griller. Then I cook my vegetables in the cast-iron frying pan, black and round as if designed for banging a recalcitrant husband on the head.

The potato goes in first, peeled and cut into 5 slices in another 10 milliliters of olive oil, because it takes the

longest time to cook. This takes 15 minutes. Carrot next: 1, peeled and cut into 10 slices. Onion: 1, also 10 slices. This is difficult with onions so I cut it across the middle to make 2 hemispheres, then 4 cuts on each half downward because attempting to make 10 equal rings is close to impossible. My knife is very sharp, professionally done at the butcher's shop in Glenferrie Road every 100 days. They think I'm a diligent but incompetent chef.

Zucchini: 1, washed not peeled. 10 slices. Beans: 10, trimmed and tailed. This is the order, from the longest time required to the shortest, so I prepare each vegetable after the previous one has been added to the pan. If I do it like this, accurately but with leisurely attention, I add the beans 10 minutes after I begin. Then I turn the chicken, set the table with a knife, fork, place mat, napkin and glass of water and by the time I come back to the stove everything is ready. I use tongs to plate it so that the chicken is on the left with 1 tablespoon of the cooking juices spooned over it, and the potatoes are fanned on the right. The rest of the vegetables are piled in the middle. 5 shakes of the salt. I sit down to eat. It is exactly 6:30 P.M.

I have always been a slow eater. I give each mouthful the attention it deserves. Chew each mouthful 30 times, they say, and you'll never be sick. It's true. I've never been sick a day in my life.

It's a slow Saturday. After my normal morning routine, I go to the café to find it almost empty. I peek in the window before I walk in. Why I'm not sure. It's not as if I can change my mind on the doorstep and go home. It's quiet as a library inside. No trouble finding a seat today. No Irishmen. No representatives of EU countries at all, as far as I can tell.

Sunday is also routine. After lunch I read the paper, alternating with a pedicure. 3 pages, trim 1 toenail, 3 pages, push back a cuticle, 3 pages, base coat, 3 pages, 1 coat of polish, 3 pages, another coat of polish, 3 pages, top coat. Then the next toe. The beauty of this system is that the time it takes to read 3 pages is exactly the time required for a coat of polish to dry.

Clean out the kitchen cupboards. Read. Now it's 8:00 P.M. 27 degrees. I am sitting by the phone, waiting for my mother's Sunday night call. My mother is a hollow, shaken woman, with skin and bones and flesh pulled taut and at the same time bowed with flapping folds. The only part of her body that holds the tiniest bit of fat is her cheeks. They are round and full like they are padded with down. She is, astonishingly, shorter than I am, and much older. She and my father were late bloomers. She wears sensible shoes, sensible hats, sensible pearls around her ridiculous neck. She is a bowerbird. Her beak and keen eyes are fierce. First

she collects her stories and then she tells them. Her mind is some kind of wall with hundreds of tiny cubicles like an old-fashioned mail room, little cubbyholes where everything is displayed for instant retrieval. How she cross-references them I'll never know. She has so many, there must be more than one wall, so perhaps each wall has wheels on its base so she can roll the walls together and then slide them apart. She needs as much storage space as she can get. She keeps stories in these cubicles, little tidbits that she collects. Blue stories for my mother, the ghoulish bowerbird.

The phone rings. It's 8:01 P.M.

"Hello, Mother."

"Hello, dear. Sorry I'm late."

"It's fine," I say. "How are you?"

"Well, my hip is giving me a little trouble, but I won't complain. I've been busy. I visited Liz across the street yesterday and we had scones with currants in them. Or were they raisins? And I've been crocheting for the stall at the community center. The azaleas are looking beautiful. I've been mulching. Mr. Parker has a rash on his tummy. I think it's the heat."

My mother's cat must be the laughingstock of all the other pets in the street. "Hey, Parker," they must sneer at him, "has your Mumsy wubbed your tummy-wummy today?"

"Perhaps he should be sleeping on the nice cold floor instead of in bed with you."

"That's funny, dear. Mr. Parker loves sleeping in my bed. Oh, and everyone asked after you at church today."

Well, that took 15 seconds. She often reaches the bit about church inside 10.

"I was speaking with Sophie . . . You remember Sophie, my next-door neighbor? Italian lady? She had that mole on her face removed last year?"

"I remember the mole . . ." It had its own postcode.

"You'll never believe what happened to her cousin's daughter's yoga teacher. She was minding her own business, driving along with her baby son in the car and she was coming down this steep hill and there were red lights at the bottom and you won't believe this, you really won't, how cruel it all is, all of it. But at the bottom of that hill of all places was a semitrailer parked at the lights and as she started down the hill the brakes went. Failed! And you know, mother of God, they slammed into the back of that semi and it squashed them flat as pancakes, both of them, never hurt anyone in their lives. It only goes to show you, we should all have four-wheel drives, not those little Japanese things. Oh, I've been meaning to ask: can sushi give you worms?"

"Have you ever eaten sushi?"

"No, dear, but I lived on kippers as a girl and they're practically the same thing."

Now that my mother has delivered her flat-as-a-pancake story she says good night. She will return this story to its cubicle so if someone at church should mention new brake pads or Japanese cars or for that matter going skiing or doing drugs or crossing the road or storms that bring down power lines or playing backyard cricket or eating sushi or buying weed killer, she'll be ready.

The real tragedy is hidden from us. Every year we pass anniversaries. We often mark them; birthdays, the day we started a job, the day we met our significant other. Our parents' wedding anniversary, name days of nieces and nephews. Lucky dates or the day we arrived in a city. The anniversary of the day the family dog died. This year will be the 27th anniversary of the day our dog died.

And every year we all pass a day, an anniversary, but we don't know the date. This is the day that might be remembered for a little while at least, and if you are very special someone might cry on this day every year or buy roses or stay in bed or go to a bar and drink their way through the top shelf starting from the left-hand side. Or if you are so environmentally unaware as

to have a tombstone, this is the date on the right-hand side. I often wonder which date will be mine.

The anniversary of my father's death is April the 21st. My father died in 1989 when I was 17, so he is spared the cubicles and their contents. He died as he lived, disappointed. His disappointment was like some kind of gas around him that left you with a bitter metallic taste in his company.

The disappointment grew around his late thirties, a realization he would never sail around the world or be best on ground for the Essendon Football Club or have a son to carry his name or start his own business in his spare room, and then, lo and behold, a feature on the front cover of *Time*. I suppose there are those people who are happy being average, living average lives, and others who despise it, rebel against it, do anything to feel different, special. My father despised it but somehow lacked the courage or the will or the reason to struggle and found himself slipping under the warm water, lulled by the movements of the waves.

He was never angry or even grumpy. He just drifted off until you could be in a room with him and still be completely alone. This freaked out the other kids on our street. Their fathers were all ruddy, explosive men, full of beer; jolly or furious, but always present. You could see through my father when the light was right

and I often found myself reaching to touch his arm, to convince myself he was real. He would startle, smile in his sheepish way and tousle my hair. When he died it was how he lived. He became paler and thinner until he was invisible, and his breathing became finer and more graceful, as if he was getting better at it instead of getting worse.

It's 8:20 P.M. Jill's turn. My sister is my polar opposite: as dark as I am fair, hair curling on her shoulders as opposed to my long straight blonde. Soft, womanly curves with a va-va-voom cleavage against my angular bones. 5 centimeters shorter. No pokey brick 6-pack flat for one, but an elegant Californian bungalow 2 streets from the beach at Hampton, a home she fills with fresh flowers and fragrant candles and the smell of roast dinners, as if her life is clipped from a decorating magazine. I always knew I wanted to teach. Jill seemed to sleep through high school, vague and barely passing, then wandered out into the world, blinking. She took a casual job at the bank, where she met Harry: older, scrambling up the corporate ladder, keen to start a family. It wasn't until she gave birth that the fog cleared for Jill. Harry Junior was a squawking, colicky child but Jill made being a mother look like Olympic ice skating. The next two, Hilary and Beth, only confirmed it. Perhaps Jill is the one who should have been

called Grace. She simmers French casseroles in a cast-iron pot and freezes the leftovers, composts food scraps for her herb garden and sews matching table runners and napkins. She also volunteers at the school cafeteria and keeps a photo of some African kiddie she sponsors on the fridge door. Phoning me each Sunday night is another of her good works.

"Hi, Gracie. Has Mum phoned?"

"Yep."

"She's not feeling too well today, Gracie. You could call her occasionally, you know. We won't have her forever."

"Uh-huh."

The clock is swinging around to 21 minutes past. Coming, coming . . . Now.

"Been doing anything?"

"Nope."

"We've been busy. Harry's going to China in a few weeks. He's been invited to speak at an international banking conference."

Really. My brother-in-law is Jill's height, 167 centimeters, and roughly her shape, complete with man-boobs. Mr. high-powered executive, too important to spend half an hour a day walking with his kids. Harry has gray wiry hair on his head that looks like it belongs in his groin, and flabby pink manicured hands. He

always wears a suit. The idea that anyone would choose to listen to Harry speak boggles the mind. A conference for Chinese insomniacs, perhaps. Or perhaps it's an IDIOT conference: International Dickheads In Overpriced Ties.

"China, huh? Are you going?"

"Thinking of it. It's only a week and the kids can stay at their friends'. I'm sure they'll be all right. It'll probably be good for them."

"Could you bring me back an abacus?"

"Of course. Hilly wants to talk to you," she says. I can hear the phone being handed over.

Hilly is my niece, Jill's middle child. I don't call her Hilly, short for Hilary, which is an egomaniacal combination of Jill and Harry. I call her Larry. Unlike Harry Junior and Beth, both of whom are chubby, dark haired and vaguely artistic like their mother, Larry resembles me at her age: all ungainly arms and legs like a newborn fawn. She's also scruffy, abhors fashion magazines and is as sharp as a tack.

"Hey." Her voice is small and thin. She's being monitored by her mother.

"Hey, Larry," I say. "How's life?"

"What do you call a tree with no leaves?"

"I don't know. What do you call a tree with no leaves?"

"A tree with no leaves."

I can hear Jill saying, "Hilly, are you telling Grace that silly tree joke?" I can hear a clunking noise as the phone is walked somewhere else, probably back to her room.

"What do you call a tree with leaves?"

I don't mind the silly tree joke. But I hope it's not a long silly tree joke.

"I don't know, Larry. What do you call a tree with leaves?"

"Russell." She chuckles in a way that is most unladylike and sounds more like me than Jill.

"Ha. That's gold, Larry. You'll have to give up on this vet idea and become a comedienne."

"I'm not going to be a vet anymore. Dad says animals get sick and die and stuff. He says I should be a teacher but that's way too boring. I'm going to be an Egyptologist."

"Really? What will your mummy think?"

"Un-funny, Grace. Did you know the Great Pyramid of Giza is the only one of the Seven Wonders of the World still left?"

"Yep. And it's made from 2.4 million blocks of stone."

Silence. "That's cool."

"How's the family?" I ask.

Some kind of clicking noise at the other end. She's playing with her iPod or Xbox or something else I don't understand. "Harry wants to drop out of the football team. Dad's gone ballistic and makes him train every day. Bethany won't leave me alone. It's so annoying. She's sleeping with a peg on her nose 'cause she thinks it's too big."

"That's gross."

"Duh. She wants a satin pillowcase like Mum's, 'cause you get less wrinkles if you sleep on satin."

"When I wake up my face looks like the Sphinx."

Snuffling noise. This amuses her. "I haven't cut your hair in ages. I did a good job last time, didn't I?"

"10 centimeters, right on the nose." Larry is one of the few people I trust. What if some distracted hairdresser removed 9.5?

"It must be really long now. When are you coming over?"

I'd like to say: Soon, honey, but I feel like I'm a planet, a serious planet like Jupiter or Saturn. It's not easy to get me out of my orbit these days.

"Mum's having some kind of lunch thing next week. It'll probably be really boring and stuff but she said you could come if you want."

I imagine Larry pulling at Jill's sleeve. "Mum, Mum, can Grace come . . . please?" until Jill says,

"All right, but you should call her Auntie Grace." This would have cost Larry something, for me.

"I'd like to, Larry, but then I'd need to have my brain Botoxed like your mother's friends."

She's sniggering. Possibly I shouldn't say things like that.

"Hold on." She's gone for a minute, or holding her hand over the phone. "Mum wants to talk to you."

"See you, DeFazio."

"See you, Feeney." She watches too much television. Cable.

Another minute and Jill is back on the phone. She's walking somewhere discreet.

"I'm having a lunch next Tuesday with some friends."

"Tuesday, did you say? Let's see. What a shame. I'm donating a kidney on Tuesday."

"Gracie. They're really nice girls. I could pick you up."

"Jill . . ."

"Okay. I wanted to talk about something else. I'm worried about Hilly."

"Uh-huh." Jill is the kind of person who worries about being hit by space junk. I cross my legs and let my foot dangle. All of a sudden I notice a wart on my foot. How could I have a wart on my foot? I don't

have contact with any humans. Can they come in the mail?

"The headmistress called last week. She's concerned about her swearing."

My tongue makes sympathetic clicking noises. "Gee, you don't expect that at a posh girls' school. Swearing headmistresses."

They're viral, I'm pretty sure.

She sighs. Perhaps she's counting to ten. "Hilly is swearing. We certainly don't talk like that at home. Harry would die if he heard her. I understand adolescents go through a rebellious stage but she's only 10. We've never had that trouble with Harry Junior."

On account of him being a total prig. I know there's a way to get rid of them . . . Put the head of a pin in a gas flame and burn them out?

"Please don't take this the wrong way . . . but . . . is it you?"

"Is what me?" Or is that for ticks?

A deeper sigh. "Are you teaching Hilly swear words?"

"Fuck no." I remember—you tie a banana skin to it.

"Grace, please!" Her voice drops to a whisper. "You have absolutely no idea what it's like to have children."

I pause for a moment. "You're quite right," I say. "I don't."

Chapter 5

Monday lunch was a disaster. I was due for an egg and salad sandwich, but I got stuck counting the sprouts. Alfalfa sprouts are the worst, even worse than grated carrot. I have gold tweezers with flat, angled points designed for eyebrows but it's hard on the back and the eyes, and easy to make mistakes. I'm normally very good at this. Not this time. When I finally got to 100 it was 2:30 P.M., way past my lunch hour, so I couldn't eat. The sandwich had to go in the trash, and then I clipped the empty plate on the edge of the fridge and it shattered everywhere. 87 pieces.

Monday was 36 degrees, Tuesday 25. I tried to do some housework despite it not being a Sunday night. I counted out 10 pieces of clothing (underpants and bras and socks and hankies don't count and are unlimited)

to make a load but I couldn't get the powder exactly level with the top of the little cup. This has never been a problem before.

There's one of my usual tasks that I don't do. I don't clean out my handbag. At the bottom of my handbag is a folded napkin. If I emptied my handbag I would have to hold the napkin in my hand, and then I might unfold it. And then I might see the phone numbers written on it. And I might never forget them.

Wednesday I think I had some kind of migraine or something, so other than the café, I stayed in bed all day. It was 14 degrees. See what I mean? It's impossible.

I have changed my routine slightly. Now I always stop 5 paces from the door of the café and peer in the window before continuing inside. It's out of my control, either way. But I'd like to be prepared.

Now it's Thursday and back to 22. At 7:00 P.M. I ring Larry. Normally I don't do this; if we speak during the week it's because she rings me. (This is okay because children can't be expected to stick to the timetable. As soon as she hits 18 things will have to change.) But I need to speak with her. So, from now on, at 7:00 P.M. on the night before any and all first dates, I ring Larry.

"So what's happening?"

"Nothing." She's sullen and terse. She's never sullen and terse.

"Come on."

"I hate Stephanie."

The joys of girlhood. I remember Jill vowing eternal sisterhood and never-ending loathing to the same girl on the same day.

"I thought Stephanie was your best friend."

"She's not. I hate her. Now my best friend's Courtney."

"What's Courtney like?"

"She's great. She's got black hair. When we leave school we're going to college together and we're going to share a flat and do anything we want. Stay up all night if we want. Have Kit Kats for breakfast if we want."

"Sounds like fun. Kit Kats contain three of the five food groups: chocolate, sugar and chocolate."

"Do you think we will? Share a flat I mean?"

"Why not?"

"Mum says I'll have a hundred more best friends before I'm 18."

Helpful. "Your mother doesn't understand. Sometimes you meet someone and your life changes forever. Remember when Nikola met Westinghouse."

"Yeah, yeah, Grace. Jeez, I know this one by heart."

Larry loves my Nikola stories. I can picture her nestling on her bed in her tribute-to-florals bedroom designed by Jill.

I sit on the couch and tuck my feet under me. "All right, Miss Brainiac. What happened?"

"When Nikola arrived in New York, he hardly had any money and he had no job. Like a backpacker. All he had was a note from his boss back in France."

"Who was the note addressed to?" I say.

"Thomas Edison. The telephone guy."

"And what did the note say?"

"Something about Nikola being the greatest?"

"Close. It said, 'I know two great men and you are one of them; the other is this young man.' Nikola was only 28 then."

"That's not young."

"I'll let that slide, considering I used to travel to school by brontosaurus."

She chuckles. "Your turn."

"Edison ripped Nikola off," I say. "Promised him a $50,000 bonus if he could redesign Edison's generators to run better. Nikola worked his guts out, barely sleeping for months."

"Poor Nikola, but he was a bit of a sucker. Daddy says always get it in writing."

That's because Daddy would rob you blind himself given half a chance.

"He was trusting. Instead of the money, Edison offered to pay him $28 a week."

"A week? I don't remember this bit. That's nothing. He must have been really pissed off."

"He was," I say.

"So Nikola told him to shove it?"

"Nikola told him to shove it," I say. "And then he met Westinghouse."

"He was an inventor too, right?"

"Yep. When he was 20, Westinghouse was nearly in a train crash. All the trains had dodgy brakes back then. He invented air brakes and made a squillion. Westinghouse already owned his own electricity company. He was a good guy. He was the first boss to give his workers a half day off on Saturdays."

"How did Nikola know they were going to be best friends?"

"Gut feeling, I guess. They couldn't have been more different, but they liked each other straightaway. Nikola was the shy, dark foreigner. Westinghouse was big and blunt with a huge coiffed mustache, always cheerful. Sometimes you've got to take the plunge, Larry. Sometimes if you open up, if you take the risk, you can achieve more, learn more, feel more with someone else. Someone you can trust, someone you can expose your heart to. Some partnerships can achieve wonderful things."

"Like me and Courtney."

"Yes. Yes, just like you and Courtney."

After I hang up I go down to the park and lie on the cricket pitch, staring up. The cement of the pitch is cool under my back. The stars are hanging right above my face. I can hear cicadas in the bushes at the side. From the noise there could be 100 of them, or 120. But there could be 2 or 3. I'll never know. How can you count what you can't see? The smell of grass and leather drifts over the oval. I'd like to stay out here all night in the quiet, but I start getting ready for bed at 9:30 P.M. and it's already 17 past 8.

Seamus Joseph O'Reilly is 38.3 years older than I am. George Westinghouse was 42, 10 years older than Nikola.

It's been years since I tried to count the stars. I spent a lot of long teenage nights staring up there trying to count them. I needed to know their number. I remember waiting until the whole house was quiet, until my parents' soft voices in the room next to mine had stopped. I remember sneaking out the window in my nightie, no slippers on my feet, and lying down in the middle of the lawn. It was cold but I didn't care. I would stare at the sky, but the fucking things move. I tried to imagine the sky as a grid, drawing lines from objects

on the ground. I tried scanning it with an aluminum-foil tube. I tried everything. Nothing works.

My favorite part in the Bible is right at the beginning, in Genesis. *And God took Abraham outside and told him to look up at the stars and count them if he could and this would be the number of his descendants.* There is a lot of counting in the Bible. Neither Mother nor Jill would realize this; they don't know much about the Bible despite, or perhaps because of, all the time they spend in church. After all, in Leviticus it says it's against the law of God to wear clothes woven from two types of material and Mother is a linen-blend kind of girl. And Exodus prohibits the charging of interest on a loan, which would be news to the pious Harry, who believes that tax deductions are God's gift to slumlords.

Why did I say yes to that Irish git? I'm due to wear a dusty pink skirt with black piping around the edges. And black wedgy heels. And a plain black T-shirt. Too girly. I might as well have "gagging for it" printed on the front. I'd rather wear jeans, and, say, a peasant top. But jeans are for winter. And although I do have a short-sleeved peasant top that fits into the spring/summer wardrobe, I had to wear it yesterday so it's not due to be worn again for another 4 to 9 days.

My last date was 2 years 6 months ago with that idiot Simon, some friend of Harry's. Jill organized it. I thought Jill said he was a Swiss baker. Interesting, I thought. Loaves with 17 different kinds of seeds. Intricate little pastries filled with chocolate. Secret recipes passed through generations of yodeling fathers and sons. All night I worried about how he would get to work by 3 A.M. to start the yeast fermenting if he kept drinking like that. By the time I realized he was a Swiss banker I was so bored I had almost lost the will to live.

But this time will be different. I'll order an entrée and one drink and then go home. To show myself I can—I can change routine if I want to. It's only that most of the time I choose not to. Luckily he suggested a place on High Street so I can walk there and walk home. We're meeting at 7:00 P.M., so if I leave at 9:05 P.M. I'll still be able to be home and start getting ready for bed on the stroke of 9:30. I can leave home at 6:40 P.M., so, counting backward: 5 minutes to put stuff in my small bag, 5 minutes to dress, 5 minutes to put on a bit of lipstick and some mascara. 5 minutes to do my hair, 5-minute shower, 5 minutes for teeth, including brushing and flossing. Start getting ready at 6:10.

The cement is chilling right inside my spine now, and the bones of my hips are tender where they touch the ground. I know it's time to head for home. The aura

of exuberance, the energy remaining from boys batting and bowling, has gone. The stars are winking but they seem very faint tonight. Light pollution from all these houses, little boxes on the hillside. I'm wasting my time even trying to count the stars because only God can do that. It says in Psalms that He decides the number of the stars. And He knows all of them by name.

When I get home from the park, despite following my normal nightly routine, I can't sleep. I lie on my bed and stare at Nikola's photo. It's not really fair to be going out without him. I'm sure he wouldn't like it. Serbians are passionate by nature—look at how upset he was when Marconi stole his patent for radio. He controlled his anger of course, and never said a bad word about anyone, but you could tell.

It's only dinner, though. It's not like I'm doing anything wrong. I remember reading somewhere that the key element of being unfaithful was secrecy. I've told him all about Seamus. This dinner's a little test for me, like an experiment. He's a scientist—he'd understand that. I've been feeling so much better lately and soon I'll be going back to work. And when I go back to work I'll have conversations with parents and eat with colleagues in the staff room. That's the thing about teaching—no matter how organized you are, how many systems you put in place, you can't plan for

people. They interrupt you. They're early. They're late. They can't get it together.

This is a trial run. Nikola would understand that.

It's Friday. 12 degrees. I don't think I can go. I'd like to. But I can't. It's already 6:02 P.M. and I have to start getting ready in 8 minutes. I'm lying on my bed, waiting for the clock to tell me it's 6:10. The trouble is my teeth ache. Mine are not sweet curvy milk teeth. My teeth are sharp with pointy canines that make me seem violent or unhinged. I'm not sure which tooth is aching. Perhaps it's not a tooth. Perhaps the ache is farther inside my jaw or in my temporomandibular joint. This makes more sense. I've looked and looked at my teeth in front of the bathroom mirror and I can't see any holes or blackening. I'm meticulous about brushing. And flossing. It probably is in the joint because my jaw is opening stiffly with a popping sensation. I've read about this. It's some kind of flaw in the tendon. I can't keep my tongue still, that's the problem. I can't keep my tongue away from each plane of each surface of each of my 28 teeth or from under the ridge below my teeth or from the back of my soft palate.

I can go. I can. It's time to start getting ready. My jaw will be okay for a few hours. The first thing I need

to do is brush and floss. I'm in the bathroom stand-
ing at the sink. My tongue doesn't know how to rest.
Where to rest. Where does it normally sit? It doesn't
lie on the bottom, flaccid. How does the saliva drain?
Do I really swallow so much, all the time? Is it always
so loud? Why would I be making all this saliva? The
saliva streams like a black river down my throat, a
dark stringing flood. If I lean forward it will fall to the
floor and curl around my foot and swell in the space
between my toes. My soles are wet. If this keeps up
I'll drown in my sleep. Why does my mouth feel so
foreign?

Oh God.

The only possible reason could be that there's
something foreign there. Because the seed of a tumor
is growing, throwing my mouth out of balance.

I once read about a man who had a tumor on his
jaw the size of an orange. It's starting here, on my jaw,
like a biblical judgment. Like I've been speaking ill of
people. Which I have, but only because they deserve it.
And now I have to take my punishment, suffer it, walk
the streets and look into people's faces knowing I'm
dying and yet they still think everything's normal. Or
the surgeons will operate and take out half my jawbone
and I won't be pretty anymore. I'll be ugly. No one will
care if I live or die. I can feel the pulse beating in my

jaw now. Probably taking secondaries to my lungs or my liver or my bones.

That's it. I'm going to bed. He'll get over it; it's not the bloody school formal. I'm not meeting his parents. He'll have a quiet dinner and go home. He doesn't have my number. I'm going to bed early and going to bed early is allowed under special circumstances, one of which is dying.

Bedtime routine begins. I pick up my toothbrush, and then I see them. No wonder. No wonder I have a tumor. I've been blind. I've been stupid.

My toothbrush is clear stiff acrylic with a softer purple rubber near the handle. The head has white and lilac nylon bristles tufting out of small holes. But how many holes? And how many bristles?

How could I not know this number? How could I never have thought to check? All those mornings. All those nights. I feel my teeth throb in time with my pulse and I remember that a pain in the jaw is sometimes the first sign of a heart attack.

15 tufts around the edge of the head. White. Down the middle are 6 rows of lilac tufts, the same height as those around the edge, interspersed with 4 rows of shorter white tufts. I sit down on the bathroom floor, shaking. My fingers are too fat to separate the bristles into individual strands. It's taking so long. Over and over I have to begin again.

34. The first tuft has 34 bristles. Strangely, so does the second.

By the time I'm about halfway through it starts getting really difficult. I realize this is because it's dark outside and I no longer have enough light to count by. Carefully, using my fingers to separate the current tuft into counted and uncounted bristles, I stretch my other arm up and hit the light.

By the time I finally raise my head, by the time all 1,768 bristles are counted and double-checked and triple-checked, my shoulders are heavy and my neck is stiff. The night is quite still.

I am quite still.

The clock tells me it is 9:24 P.M. In the restaurant, they'll be handing round the dessert menus. In my flat, it's almost time to get ready for bed. So I sit at the edge of the bath for 6 minutes and wait.

At 9:30 I stand at the sink. This time as I hold my toothbrush in my hand, I'm sure. I know how many strands of nylon brush each tooth. I can picture them. My jaw is safe. My teeth are safe.

Then I look at my toothbrush. I buy a new toothbrush on the first of every month but this one doesn't look new anymore. It's stretched and dog-eared. The bristles bend back at horrible angles, after being rifled over and over, jammed by my fingers. It looks like a toilet brush.

I can't put this in my mouth.

I can't go to sleep without brushing my teeth.

I must start getting ready for bed at 9:30 P.M. and it's already 9:30 P.M.

I must buy a toothbrush on the first of the month and it's not the first of the month.

I force a deep breath in, then out.

I now know that there are 1,768 bristles and I doubt there's another person alive outside of a toothbrush factory who knows that. This is what will happen. As it's a Friday night, not a school night, I will start getting ready for bed at 10:30 P.M. instead of 9:30. I will do this in the future on all Friday and Saturday nights. Even though there are 7 days until the first of the month, I will buy 2 new toothbrushes—1 until the end of the month and 1 to start next month with. This mid-month change in toothbrushes will only occur when I count the bristles. In fact I'll walk to the supermarket now and buy as many toothbrushes of this kind as I can because if they discontinue this model and introduce a new model I'll have to count the bristles all over again.

I don't need my usual leaving-the-house ritual because this isn't a shopping trip—this is an extension of my new ritual for the night I run out of toothbrushes, so I can simply grab my keys and purse and walk. I go

in what I'm wearing: gray tracksuit pants many sizes too big that belong in my drawer labeled "comfy." (The label is on the inside of the drawer.) Sneakers, dark blue. Big sweatshirt, navy, also comfy. T-shirt. Black. Hair pulled back in a ponytail. No makeup.

At the grocery store I take a green basket and fill it with all the toothbrushes of my brand and type that they have. 14. The colors don't matter but they must be medium, not soft or hard, otherwise the number of bristles might not be the same.

He's wearing calico pants and a chambray shirt. His hair is dry this time. He's buying half a roast chicken, mutilated by the girl with the kitchen shears, and some exhausted vegetables. His shirt is tucked into his pants and I can see the tail of it bunched up near his bottom.

It's when I'm walking to the checkout that I see him.

I can only see his back but it's him.

It's like I can smell him.

He can't smell me.

I need to be still. Maybe if he turns around, he won't see me.

He turns around.

He sees me.

Chapter 6

I sleep in a single bed because I have a horror of the vast expanse of doubles. Before my sister's wedding we stayed, each bridesmaid in her own room, in a five-star hotel in the city filled with gamblers and couples. The bed was a king-size, designed for those enormous American kings, and I lay still all through that long night because each movement of my legs broke new cold ground. I never knew for certain where the edge was.

In my own single bed, I know. I know its width and length in hand spans and kicks and there is no spot so far from my body that it cannot feel the heat of my blood. A double bed is a dare, a question. A single bed is complete with just me in it. A double bed is a vacant promise. A threatening Miss

Havisham. The thought of having one in my house makes my lower back ache. I wouldn't know how to lie in it.

That's how I feel right now. I thought I knew this supermarket. I certainly know its dimensions in steps. The width of its aisles. But now that he's looking at me I'm adrift. I can't think of a rule to follow. His presence distorts the walls. They've moved now. The air has ripples through it.

We're standing 5 paces apart. Or would be if the world was still the same.

"Dinner," he says, gesturing to his basket.

"Oh," I say.

"I'm absolutely starving."

There's no emotion on his face. No anger. No surprise.

He continues. "I usually eat earlier than this."

"I see."

"But tonight I've been flat out. I've got a new hobby. Memorizing menus."

"Look, Seamus . . ." It's too hard to tell him I've had more important things to worry about.

"It was a good one, too. Risotto pescatora, spaghetti marinara, spaghetti della nonna. That's chicken meatballs. Even fettuccine calabrese, with extra chili, the way I like it. One day I'll have to eat there."

The rest of the supermarket has faded away. He's taking up all the space. "Look, Seamus, something came up."

His face turns pink. Amazing that can happen so fast. "You could have told me if you didn't want to come. You could have called. Or sent me a text."

It's true. I could have called him or sent a text. But that would have meant opening the napkin and reading his numbers, and punching them into the phone. And then his numbers would have stuck in my memory, become a part of me so that years from now I might still remember the 10 numbers of Seamus.

"It was nothing like that. I didn't feel well. Really suddenly."

He blinks and his lips purse into a half smile, yet he doesn't avoid my eyes. His voice is soft. He nods. "It's okay. You don't have to say that. Life is a series of maybes and what-ifs."

The lights in the supermarket are too bright. Everything around me is hard surfaces, shiny floor, beaming glass. He is not hard or shiny or beaming. He's soft and frowning. And he's right. Life is a series of maybes and what-ifs. Suddenly I wish I had met him at the restaurant. I wish I'd had risotto pescatora and a glass of red wine and shared a tiramisu and sat and talked with Seamus Joseph O'Reilly until they packed up the

chairs around us. Suddenly it seems rather an important thing to have missed.

"I'm so—"

"God. You really do live in a house filled with supermodels."

He's looking down at my basket. I swing it behind my back. "Not really. Really I'm an amateur toothbrush designer. These are for research."

He smiles, this time with his eyes. The skin around his temples relaxes. "So you're either a supermodel, some kind of apocalyptic bulk shopper or a frustrated oral health stylist."

"Or all of the above. Or perhaps my hobby is collecting personal-care products. Star Wars dolls, Princess Diana plates . . . they bore me. These babies'll be worth a fortune in a few years."

I realize I've said this to make him smile.

Somehow the stillness that is in the store is now inside me as well. Stillness races through my veins instead of blood. My body feels light, my hands, my face.

"I'll give it another try if you will." It's only when I hear this that I realize it's my voice speaking. It's only when I see his face that I realize I mean it. I gesture to his basket. "I haven't eaten."

Chicken and vegetables. For a change.

He is quiet for a long time. "Let's aim a bit lower. Is your car outside?"

I shake my head. "I walked."

"What if I walk you home? If you'd like." He pauses for a moment and bites his lower lip with his front tooth. The left one. It leaves a dent.

"I'd like."

He looks politely at the chewing gum and chocolate bars as I go through the checkout with 14 toothbrushes. He pays for his half chicken and vegetables. We go outside. It's quiet except for a boy collecting shopping trolleys, coasting on them, squeaking, from under the streetlight where they'd been deserted. Seamus reaches across me to take my plastic bag of toothbrushes. A well-brought-up boy. Chivalrous. His fingers take the 2 white plastic straps from mine. His fingers are not mine. Are different from mine, so different I'm amazed that he also has 10. I notice the size of his hands. Their color. The tiny pale hairs on the back of his fingers.

We reach the corner before I realize I've forgotten to count the steps.

The mathematician and engineer Charles Babbage, inventor of the first computer, got it. When he read Tennyson's poem "The Vision of Sin," he was most upset.

He was so upset he sent Tennyson a letter. It went:

"Every minute dies a man, Every minute one is born"; I need hardly point out to you that this calculation would tend to keep the sum total of the world's population in a state of perpetual equipoise, whereas it is a well-known fact that the said sum total is constantly on the increase. I would therefore take the liberty of suggesting that in the next edition of your excellent poem the erroneous calculation to which I refer should be corrected as follows: "Every moment dies a man, And one and a sixteenth is born." I may add that the exact figures are 1.167, but something must, of course, be conceded to the laws of metre.

I know this letter by heart, and as I leave the supermarket next to Seamus I think each syllable with my footfall but I don't count. All the way home I don't count. The street is empty and it's been raining. The water makes the tram tracks shine in the streetlamps and we don't speak. A car goes past. And another. We don't speak. A third splashes some water onto my feet. He stops, takes my arm and maneuvers me so I am no longer walking on the street side. He puts me on the inside.

Charles Babbage definitely got it. Most people don't. They don't understand that numbers rule, not just the world in a macro way but their world, their own world.

Their lives. They know that $E=MC^2$ because they heard it in school or it was the answer to a quiz show question. They don't really understand what it means: that matter and energy are the same thing. That their skinny latte and iPod and nipple ring are all energy, little packets of energy constrained very close together. That everything and everybody are connected by a mathematical formula.

Would Seamus get it if I told him?

At the lights he pushes the walk button. This is the only time it's awkward, right now, waiting for the lights to change.

"Have you lived here long?" He turns toward me as he speaks.

"Forever. Prahran or Brunswick would be groovier, I know, but I like the spaces. I like the spaces between the people better than the people themselves." The green man appears. The beeps begin. I sound like an idiot.

He frowns. "Space. Everyone needs space."

As we walk I realize our pace is almost identical although he is taller. He is slowing his gait to match mine. I take a deep breath. "Sometimes I feel my thoughts can't properly develop if they run into another person as soon as they're born. They need room to work out exactly what shape to take."

We've been walking for at least 10 or 11 minutes and he's said almost nothing. Walking these streets together, it feels like we're in church. I fight the urge to whisper. There's no wind. I hear nothing but cars on High Street, shushing through puddles, and the sound of our steps. We're so quiet we surprise a possum on a light pole. We keep walking. You mind your business, we'll mind ours.

We walk down the side street now and we've reached the spot where I need to make a decision. I need to lean across him and take my bag of toothbrushes back, if that's what I'm going to do. I can do it easily; I can say, "Thanks, officer. I can take it from here," or "I don't want to take you out of your way," or "Did I mention I have a communicable disease?"

But I don't. Instead, at the corner I stop and say, "So are you planning to polish off an entire half chicken by yourself?"

He lifts the hand with the bags in it. "This miserable runt? I think it's a tall quail. And 3 petrified potatoes and a bit of soggy pumpkin. This isn't exactly what I had in mind when I invited you to dinner."

I lean back against the lamppost and cross my arms. "Luckily we supermodels don't eat much."

He smiles into my eyes, and bows. "In that case, my quail is your quail."

As we walk up the path, I think of Nikola and West-inghouse. How different they were. How perfect for each other. Westinghouse bought 40 patents, includ-ing the induction motor he desperately needed, from Nikola for a complicated blend of cash, royalties and shares. Nikola left New York and moved to Pittsburgh to help Westinghouse overcome any difficulties in the manufacture of the motor. No regrets. No fear.

At the top of the stairs I fumble for my keys in the pocket of my track pants. We go inside. My last proper visitor was in October of the year before last when Larry slept over, on the couch. Jill and Harry had gone for a skiing weekend. I'd like to think they had in fact gone to a mad 3-day key party in a lodge with a spa, 6 cans of whipped cream, 1 midget and 1 latex Batman suit but, knowing them, it probably was a skiing week-end. Having Larry here felt right—we watched the late movie until past her bedtime, had ice cream for dinner and made crank calls to a boy she liked at school. Having Seamus here is different.

"This is it," I say. "My lair. It's here I hatch my plans for world domination. I'm saving for a white Persian and a monocle."

"Nice. No supermodels or bomb shelters, I notice." He puts the chicken, vegetables and my toothbrushes on the kitchen counter. He opens the bag and riffles

through them. "So, Grace. Are you going to tell me why you've bought so many toothbrushes?"

I pretend to think for a moment and fold my arms. "Ah . . . No."

He shrugs. "Fair enough."

His hands are in his pockets and he leans his left hip against the counter. My flat is made for me, measured for me, for the length of my tibia and fibula and ulna and spine. His bones are longer than mine and if I lined my limbs and back and fingers up against his I would find a difference in length and also in thickness. The room is out of proportion now, like long hair on a baby or a mansion surrounded by one meter of lawn and a high fence. He takes up all the room.

There's no space now for my thoughts to develop and they fall stillborn onto my dark green carpet. Now, I do understand $E=MC^2$. I understand that the little packets of energy that are my thoughts have become matter. A solid body. Flesh.

Chapter 7

S ometime the next day or the one after that, I kiss
him. Or maybe it is 2 minutes after we walk in
the door. I am still standing in my kitchen and he is
still leaning on my kitchen counter, hands in pockets.
I move my body across until it is close to his. My kiss,
this first one, is more a pressing, lips closed and soft.
For one instant he is still. For one instant I think that
there is nothing I can say to erase such a foolish act.
Then he moves toward me. He trails his closed mouth
across my top lip so I can feel the tiny prickles. His
mouth brushes along the line of my jaw and scoops up
the side of my face. Along my eyebrow. My left eye-
brow. He licks my eyes closed. His tongue is pointed.

His hands come out of his pockets and cup my face
while he kisses my mouth. The inside of his mouth

seems too soft for a man, so soft that I wonder how he chews, how he bites the ends of pens without lacerating it. His mouth is warm. He knows how to kiss.

This skin near my hip is cold against his hand. His hair is soft, threaded through my fingers. He pulls up my sweatshirt, and my T-shirt under that, and his fingers are so much darker than my skin that I seem brand new. He does not seem afraid of my body. He does not scan my moles to see if the edges bleed into the skin around them, and his fingers smooth my flesh but do not check for lumps that should not be there, waiting under the surface.

He can't want me.

I should have worn a bra. I should have worn a red lace bra, something French or designed by a singer. But I don't own anything like that. I should have thought this out a bit more carefully and waxed or at least shaved my underarms. Is my deodorant still working from this morning? His left hand has found my right breast; it is cold and quite rough for someone with a desk job. He pauses for a moment. He exhales; perhaps he is also disappointed that I'm not wearing a red lace bra. Or perhaps I look panicked, like a woman who's only had 5 lovers in her entire life and none at all for 3 years come April 6. He frowns and swallows and tilts his head so that our foreheads touch.

"We can...would you rather...How about something to eat? That chicken won't age well."

I shake my head. I lean forward and kiss the side of his throat.

He bends his head back a little and groans. Now he kneels and I can feel his lips and tongue on my side, sliding around toward my navel. The trace his tongue leaves behind is cold when the air hits it. Then he says, "Get down here."

I kneel down so that I am almost eye-level with him. He has both my breasts in his hands now. Please, God, don't let him take off my sweatshirt. He'll see they're not even, that my breasts are not even. The left one hangs down lower than the right. 5 millimeters. My collar bones aren't even either. They don't align. One sticks out farther than the other. No reason—not a legacy of a childhood accident. No genetic deformity passed from mother to daughter like a bone china tea set. Misaligned, that's all. Surely when he sees that he'll stop. He'll give up.

He doesn't give up. When he takes my sweatshirt off over my head he doesn't seem to notice the misalignment and doesn't seem to measure my breasts at all, either with his eyes or with his hands. I try to count his kisses, the little nips as his front teeth graze the underside of my breasts, but then he takes my nipple in his

mouth, and, oh, I can't count. Not a number will go through my mind. It's deathly still in here. I haven't even had a chance to open the window since I arrived home. I can't even think about what the time is, about what time I'm supposed to be in bed, about how unhygienic it is to be lying on the kitchen floor with this man sucking my breasts.

All I can feel is a small thin line, like an electric cable sparking, burrowing through my flesh hot and cold, from my nipple to between my legs. The taste of him is in my mouth and in the air and in my hair. The taste of him is under my nails and wherever he kisses me he will taste only himself.

Looking back, what's hardest to believe is what he didn't notice and what he did. He didn't seem to notice that my tummy has a little rounded bulge. But he did notice the thick white scar on my right knee from when I fell off my bike when Mrs. Jennings's dog was chasing me. He kissed it and bit it. I'm sure he noticed my pubic hair needed a trim, because at one point he wound his fingers through it and gently ground his knuckles into the padded part of me until I could feel a slick wetness on the top of my thighs and I knew I could no longer bear his touch.

When he fucked me he started off very patient, very slow, and only when I started begging did he speed up.

I felt my orgasm begin a long way away as a kind of stillness encroaching on my whole mind and body. Soon he could feel my muscles squeezing and shivering and he held me tighter and kissed my neck. It started small and shy but at the end I tried to pull away because it's all too much, too much feeling, too much tensing. My back arched. My thighs squeezed him. It's always like this, but I don't always have a heavy body trapping me with the sensation. This time there was no escaping. This time it went on and on.

I didn't notice how many strokes he took or how many times he said my name. The numbers scattered from my fingertips and ran across the floor. I was pinned under him and could not chase them.

After we finish and catch our breath, the cold of the kitchen floor tightens my skin. His semen is smeared on my thighs. His semen is on the floor too, in a series of rounded droplets, some large and some small. The edges are crinkling, already starting to coagulate. It does this so it's less likely to run out of a vagina before it's done its job. After a while it liquefies again so the happy sperm can swim until they find their egg. I'd never noticed how beautiful semen is. It's pearlescent, and slippery like skin lotion. It's warm from being inside his body and mine. I should clean it up before someone takes a fall.

I pull my tracksuit pants up and pull my top back down. I refuse to think about how I look, or about the stains on my pants. I'm not feeling self-conscious; too late for that. Only a little cold. He buttons his shirt and pulls his underpants up. I don't know if this was because I did or because he was cold too. I take his hand and lead him to my bedroom. He doesn't seem to notice I only have a single bed. He doesn't say one word and his eyes never leave me. His shoes and trousers are still in the kitchen. He is wearing only his shirt and underpants when he lies down, and he falls asleep almost straightaway, curved with space for me to sleep beside him. I lie down next to him without brushing my teeth, or flossing, or changing into my pajamas or washing my face or making a cup of tea or putting my slippers beside the bed or rearranging my pillows. If he noticed how tight I was or how quickly I came, he didn't say anything.

Every night I lie between these sheets but now I feel the weave and the coolness and the tension of each strand of cotton. I can feel him down the back of my head, and down my neck, and down each centimeter of my spine, and across my coccyx and around the curve of my bottom and down the back of my legs and the hollow of my knee and the length of my calves. My toes tingle like currents are dancing on the surface of my

skin. Like a wire has unwound from the socket near the floor, has arced to the leg of the bed and now my body is covered in a million tiny bursts.

The first electric chair was made using Nikola's technology. Perhaps the chair feels like this, at the beginning. Perhaps the electricity starts like a warm glow. Maybe it grows stronger until it feels like ants crawling, then stronger again until it feels like bees stinging. Then, only then, does it feel like electrocution.

The first man to die in the electric chair was William Kemmler, a petty criminal who killed his girlfriend with an ax. His electrocution was not Nikola's doing. He and Westinghouse fought against it in the courts. Electricity was too unpredictable, they said. It was Edison who arranged the first electric chair to show that Nikola's type of electricity, AC, was deadly and that DC current, the one Edison promoted, was safe.

Kemmler was strapped into a chair and 2 electrodes were attached to his body: the first on his head and the second his spine. The machine began. The dials rose. The executioner directed the flow of electricity through Kemmler.

I wonder how Nikola and Westinghouse felt at exactly that moment. Everything they had worked for, everything that they believed in, was on the brink of ruin. No one in their right mind would want AC

electricity in their home, around their children, near their wives. They would be trying to sell a product that killed people. Perhaps they were at Westinghouse's home. He was a physical kind of man, so maybe he stood there with his hand on Nikola's shoulder, both of them thinking their dream had died. Maybe the blackness that flowed through Nikola's heart when the electricity flowed through Kemmler's body was lessened by Westinghouse's being there. Maybe Nikola also felt he was no longer alone.

The electricity on my skin doesn't come from a chair or from my bed. Nikola is looking down on me, but it doesn't come from him either.

It is amazing that I sleep. It is not so amazing that it is 4:07 A.M. when I wake. 4 is the worst time to wake, as anyone with the normal human sensitivities will tell you. Far too late to make a cup of tea or to go back to sleep. Far too early to get up and do something constructive. There's nothing on television but arrogant evangelists and people selling acne solutions and motivational tapes. For me, base 12 philosophy aside, midnight is not the witching hour. 4:00 is.

Up until this point, I slept beautifully. And for an instant when I wake I think: This is what happens to normal people. They can go to bed without flossing

10 times up and down between each tooth or rearranging their 10 pillows if they choose, and they can still sleep deep and wide. And I wake like I am still in a dream, in the arms of a handsome man who has just made love to me, and free to decide when and how I go to bed. In the shape of a spoon with Seamus curved at the back of me. But I wake up thinking of numbers.

Not dates or days. Not phases of the moon. Not my ovulation date. I'm on the pill. Have been for 19 months. Not that there's been any likelihood of sex until now, just because I can't bear not knowing when my period is due. I was never horribly irregular—some poor women don't know if it's a 14-day cycle, or 28, or if it's coming at all. That would send me certifiable. I was somewhere between 26 and 30 but now it's like clockwork, every 28 days.

So I'm not worried about being impregnated by the 50,000,000 sperm per normal ejaculation of between 2 and 5 milliliters of semen. 50,000,000-ish. Depending on how long it's been since he's had sex. With someone else. Before now.

The numbers I wake up worrying about are statistics. 40,000,000 people worldwide have HIV. More than 3,000,000 people die every year. 60 percent of all HIV infections are from vaginal intercourse.

Not to mention chlamydia. Gonorrhea.

I refuse to be one of those germ-fearing crazies. Bacteria are everywhere, and they're mostly good and they stimulate your immune system. People with no exposure to germs get cancer. Everybody knows that.

But unprotected sex on the kitchen floor with a man I barely know?

I would have asked the question on the walk home if I'd realized things were heading this way. I could have said, "So, given blood lately?" or "Had a physical?" or "Any recent anal sex I should know about?"

His arm is becoming heavy and his breathing is blowing my hair. He does look a little pale. The tops of my thighs are sticky.

Whatever the disease is, I've probably got it. And not because of the sex.

It was the unflossing and the unbrushing and the unwashing and no tea. No place for my slippers, no order for my pillows. In the dark I can see my pajamas waiting accusingly on the chair in my bedroom. These are not small, these wrongs disguised as nothings. They are somethings. They are tiny cracks in the world that run for miles underground. They cause earthquakes and landslides and in my mind I see the kind of people who suffer in disasters like these; an old woman, perhaps, or motherless children, wide eyes turned to a photographer they hope will tell the world

and then someone stronger will come and lift them up. I can almost feel a tremor now as I lie here because I know this arm and this bed and this room and this house and this earth are not stable. There is nothing solid here and it will all crack and split and I will fall into the ground and there will be nothing but the fall and nothing solid not even an end to this crevice. And the worst is the knowledge that it is me. It is me who has shaken it. My foolish, stupid forgetting.

This is the world we live in; it's cruel, endlessly cruel and unstable and accidents are everywhere and we can never escape them. Your pet could die or some stupid careless child cause never-ending grief with some small thoughtless act. People die, children die, through no fault of their own. When I think of the unraveling of my world I want to cry, and I start to cry, and I cry silently because I do not want him waking and asking me about my tears. My body starts to quiver from holding in my sobs and my breath comes in small snorts through my nose but I am still almost silent.

Is my mother all right? I suddenly know that she is not all right, she is dying, right now, lying on the bathroom floor with her stick arms outstretched, clawing, and she is calling my name to come and help her die. She dropped her hair dryer in the bath then reached in to get it; a piece of bread was stuck in the toaster

and she levered it out with a knife. When I was 6 I had a fever and she stayed with me and sat on my bed and fed me vanilla ice cream with a silver spoon from the set she used only for company. The feeling of lying ill, the air torpid, crickets singing, aluminum venetians drawn in a vain attempt to close out the heat that seemed to fill my every inch. I was as light as air then; I drifted away and I could almost see my own body on my bed from where I rested on the ceiling. I heard my mother's soft footsteps, doing something inconsequential—folding laundry, sweeping. Breaking eggs. A sound that brought me back to my bed, tucked me in and kissed my forehead. I remember a thousand small gifts of her love, unthanked and unrepaid. And she is dying now because of me.

Or maybe it's Jill. Maybe I'm feeling Jill's death. She is younger than I am so it would be some kind of fall; people die all the time in falls, crack their heads open. Or a car smash, perhaps 2 or 3 hours ago but no one's thought to call me until now because they've been so busy trying to push life back inside her, handsome people in white yelling, "Intubate now!" or "Type B stat!" It would be because of that fuckhead Harry; they would have gone to some tedious function for his job and he's been drinking and it's up to her to drive. She's not a good driver, too timid, too nervous, and I

don't think that a car the size of a small flat helps. It was probably raining—that's rain I can hear outside—and in the dark she's misjudged the right-hand turn at the lights and a black sedan, ridiculous color in this weather, has run the yellow and smashed into the driver's side. Her side. Harry's only shaken of course, the other driver's okay and she's crushed. I know she is. Her body is broken and her face is mauled.

With Jill gone, there's so much missing. The games we used to play when we were little are gone now. We used to play a game where we picked our future husbands and then practiced writing our new names. Designing our future life. From when she was 10 she would pick some rock star; she'd know everything about him—middle name, favorite food, everything—from the fan magazines and I knew nothing about anyone except characters from books, so my husbands would vary: Simon Templar, Peter Wimsey, Ellery Queen. I would convince her these were real boys who liked me, boys who lived just a suburb over, and she, as the smaller one, would not think to question me. Back then her eyes would grow wider when she looked at me, as though the 3 extra years gave me wisdom. And I have done nothing but damage her.

All the games will die with her. Larry will have no mother and I will try to take her hand at the funeral

but she will pull away from me and in her eyes will be the knowledge that it was me and I will never be able to be a mother to her.

I have destroyed everything, held it in my hand and crushed it and there is no recovering from this, none, none none none none none.

Arm is really heavy on me now not moving lying pressing. Not moving not breathing. He could be dead I don't know him don't really heart disease asthma some kind of stroke. Aneurism popping in his brain small vital clot. He could be still and turning cold blue I could be pinned who do I call his dead skin touching mine rubbing spreading dead. No movement. Chest still. Can't turn to see. Are his eyes open staring dead. Lying next to me. Decomposing.

"Ssshh . . . It's all right, it's all right . . ."

I jump through the air at least 5, maybe 5.3 centimeters.

"It's all right, Grace. You're having a nightmare." His voice is creased with waking and concern. He pats my hair twice, touches my face.

Breathe. Perhaps I am. Perhaps I am having a nightmare.

"Wake up, Grace. God, you're shivering. And panting like you've run a marathon. You're all right." His voice is lower now, and his words are like cooing. He

stops patting me, and now he holds me. Too tight to be a normal hug. Tight like he wants me to know that he's here. Like he wants to hold all of my body in his arms. He keeps telling me I'm all right. He sounds very confident.

"God, that must have been a shocker. You feel like ice. Come on. Let me hold you."

He's already holding me. His flesh is burning my cold skin. Hold me.

"Tell me about it. Trust me, it fades quicker if you tell me about it. I know about nightmares. When I was a kid I used to dream there were snakes living under my bed, and they'd come out in the middle of the night and crawl all over me. I'd wake my parents, screaming the house down. Come on, Grace. What was it?"

Maybe he's right. Everyone has nightmares, even Seamus. Maybe this was just a regular nightmare, the kind that happens to normal, regular people, and I just dreamed I was awake. How many snakes were living under his bed? Only 2? Or 2,000?

I want it to stop. I want it all to stop.

Suddenly I'm sick of it. Sick of counting all the time. Of all the little games and rules and orders and lists and chewing my food 30 times and drinking a cup of tea before bed every night. I want to have a job and go to the movies and have a family and people over for a

dinner that is not chicken and vegetables. I want to be like everybody else. I want to run as fast as I can in bare feet and on grass like I'm a child and my hair is streaming behind me. I want to run and I want to feel my leg muscles stretch and pull and my chest heave in the service of my freedom.

I don't want to count anymore.

"My mother. And Jill. Dead," I manage.

"Who's Jill?"

His eyes narrow and are surrounded by little crinkles of concentration, caused by too much UV exposure. He's the kind of man who goes outside without sunscreen on. He can drive a car. He can leave his house without knowing where he's going, and he can take a trip with no itinerary. He could probably go to a restaurant and order food he feels like eating; he wouldn't need to order the first meal in alphabetical order or the first item on the first page of the menu or any one of a dozen other systems I've tried. He knows what it feels like to run fast.

"My little sister." It's fading fast, this nightmare, and the closer he holds me the faster it fades.

"What happened? Grace?"

Chapter 8

Tell him. He's holding me and he wants to know. "She died and Mother died. They both died horrible deaths and I should have looked after them and it's all my fault."

I meet his lovely, crinkly eyes and, although I'm feeling much better, mine fill with tears. He pulls me closer until we are pressed together in my single bed and his limbs enfold mine because they are delightfully longer. His legs are maybe 8 or 9 centimeters longer than mine, his arms maybe 4 or 5. It's difficult to be accurate from this angle. I have a soft tape measure on my bedside table next to the photo of Nikola that I use to check the placement of the furniture every week, but it's a little hard to reach for it now. His lips brush my forehead and my hair, and my face becomes pressed

against his neck. It's beautiful in here, warm. It smells kind.

He murmurs in a soft voice like he's comforting a child. "Listen to me, Grace. Grace, sweetheart. It's a bad dream, that's all. No one's dead, and no one's going to die."

The room is growing pale as the day arrives; it filters through my lace curtains and flicks across the floor. That first half-light lifts my skin and his face and the room seems a different place. The night seems a long way away. Another country. I can hear the birds beginning to sing outside, but it's still too early for traffic. Seamus is all confidence, lying in my bed in my flat, holding me like I belong to him. He's a man whose nightmares come only at night. A man who can ask about my toothbrushes and grin and shrug and say, "Fair enough," when I keep my secret.

Seamus smiles at me. "No one's number's up while I'm here."

The next time I wake, the lightness inside my lids tells me the sun is up, and the air is still instead of moving. My eyes are closed, and my mind and my body are still. I am in my childhood bedroom.

I feel the angle of the bed from the way the sun falls. I can smell the ironed clothes hanging in the closet. The

sheets are flannelette, not crisp cotton. If I opened my eyes I'd see my china figurines. Yet there is one thing that brings me back to the present, a smooth brown arm curled around my waist. After my nightmare, I must have fallen asleep again in those arms.

I open my eyes. On my bedside table, Nikola is looking down at me. The night before the killing of Kemmler, Nikola probably woke at 4:00 A.M., perhaps in panic as I did, and perhaps like me he saw only death around him. The next morning, August 6, 1890, at 6:00 A.M., Kemmler would die, smoothly and cleanly as Edison had promised. All Nikola had thought of and dreamed of would finish. No one would ever want AC power in their home.

But it didn't finish. Because Kemmler didn't die cleanly.

As soon as the electricity coursed through his skin and nerves and vessels, Kemmler began to pull at the ties that bound him, stretching them in anguish until they came close to breaking. He screamed too, a sound that stabbed the ears of those who hailed electricity as a new era in humane killing. After 17 seconds the current was switched off.

I wish I could have been with Nikola that dark night. I wish I could have told him, "Pay no attention to your fears. The scent of death may be upon you, and it may

be upon your dreams, but it will not kill your vision."
Perhaps I would even have held him and said, "Your
number's not up, Nikola. Not while I'm here."

Kemmler was still alive, horribly injured and writh-
ing, his bladder and bowels and balls emptying in front
of the appalled witnesses.

The executioner decided to switch the generator
on for another burst, but they had to wait until it re-
charged. They were forced to wait as Kemmler con-
vulsed and gasped. This time the current ran through
his body again for almost a minute and by the end the
air in the small room was thick with the smell of burn-
ing flesh and smoke was rising from Kemmler's scalp.

"They would," Westinghouse said later, "have done
better using an ax."

Perhaps not the next morning, but soon after the
execution, Edison's power over the future of electric-
ity began to wane. Despite the terror in the night, de-
spite the horrible dreams of death, perhaps it didn't
take long for Nikola's faith in his vision to return, and
a sense of certainty about his future to fill him again.
Nikola would have slept more soundly, resting like he
was again a child. Like the man beside me.

"Seamus." I mouth his name. I know he is awake,
but his breathing is long and even and his eyes are
closed.

He is on his left side, against the wall, so close to me in my single bed that with my head turned toward him he takes up my entire field of vision. I am on my back, one of his arms under my neck and the other across my body below my breasts. His blondish hair looks darker now, pressed down against his scalp. His forehead is high and smooth. His eyebrows are unruly, and underneath his eyes are puffy bags. His nose is a fraction too big for his face, and between his nose and his lips the indentation is deep to match the dimple in his chin. His morning shadow is darker than his hair.

I want to kiss every cell.

Instead I take a deep breath in, and let it out in a sigh. "I need to tell you something."

"Hmmm?" His eyes are still closed.

"My name is Grace Lisa Vandenburg," I say, still staring at the ceiling. "I am 35 years old. My mother is Marjorie Anne, and my sister Jill Stella is 33. Jill is married to Harry Venables; he's 40 on the second of May. They have three children: Harry Junior is 11, Hilary is 10 and Bethany is 6. My father's name was James Clay Vandenburg, and he died 17 years, 5 months and 17 days ago. I have a science degree and a Dip.Ed. I lost my virginity in my first boyfriend's car outside my mother's house. I don't like coriander. I don't like realist paintings. Why don't people take a photo if they want realism? I love abstract paintings. Once I went to

"Late, shmate. Should I be worried?"

"No. Should I worry about a little half-Irish half-supermodel surprise in nine months' time?"

"I'm on the pill."

He stretches like a cat, then turns on his side and unhooks my fingers from around the sheet. He holds my hand flat and kisses the pulse point of my wrist, tracing with his lips and teeth a line down to my inner elbow. "I do feel a bit guilty," he says.

He feels guilty? Nikola is staring at me in bed with an usherette I've known for 15 days and he feels guilty? My God. He's got a wife. 10 kids. My hands make fists, nails burrowing into my palms. "Why?"

He sits on the edge of the bed. I scoot my body away. "I promised you Italian. No Italian. Then I promised you gourmet supermarket quail, and still nothing. No dinner at all. You must be starving." In an instant he vaults over me, landing lightly on his feet on the floor. "I have a great idea. How about breakfast? Something unrelentingly bad for you, like bacon or eggs Benedict or pancakes or preferably all 3. Then you can tell me more things. Childhood illnesses, favorite music, your football team—whatever you like."

I look up at the ceiling. I've got so many things to do. I need to wash my hair and dry it and brush each section 100 times, then dress. And Saturday mornings

are for shopping. I have to brush my teeth and wash my face and I've missed the alarm already but that doesn't mean the day is ruined. I can start again at the beginning of the next hour.

"That is . . . I mean . . . if you're free . . ."

"It's not that."

He takes my hands and holds them together by the wrists. He brings them close to his body so I have no choice but to look into his eyes. "Grace, I have something very important to ask you. Please don't think I'm asking this lightly. Please think about it, carefully, before you answer."

I tense my shoulders, my hands.

"Grace, can I have one of your toothbrushes? I'd really like to brush my teeth but I'd hate to leave you short. For . . . whatever."

I laugh. I'll pretend the supermarket had one less. "You may."

"Thanks. Now, I'm going to the toilet. Then I'm going to brush my teeth with a specimen from your collection. I'm going to put on my clothes from last night, as unappealing as that sounds. Then I'm taking you out for breakfast, because we need food and we need coffee. Okay?"

The air is even more still now than it was before. It's early. The day is brand new. This morning, I have

woken up with someone else in my bed. Last night, I did not do my nighttime routine. The day is new, and it is filled with possibilities and I am filled with possibilities. He barely knows me. I can be anyone I want.

"Well?" he asks again.

Get up. Go to the bathroom. Brush my teeth with a new toothbrush. Put on clothes from last night. Go for breakfast.

The way he said it like that, it sounds like a list.

I pull myself out of bed with a determination and suddenness that surprises me. I stand next to the bed. I'm up.

"No."

His eyebrows rise satisfactorily.

"No, I have no football team. Marx was wrong. Sports are the real opium of the people."

He grins, as wide a grin as I've ever seen, and the crinkles around his eyes look like lots more smiles. "That's sad, Grace. That's really sad. But it might not be your fault. Perhaps you need to be shown the beauty in a run down the wing, or a long goal from the boundary."

I take two toothbrushes from the bag and throw him one. "Football? Please. Why do people care? And 6 points for 1 goal? That's just plain annoying. Why

does their team, an arbitrary, illogical grouping at best, inspire this kind of boneheaded loyalty?"

I'm in the bathroom with the door closed, but he keeps talking. "It's not arbitrary. It's far from arbitrary." I can hear other noises, too. Kitchen cupboards, opening and closing. The fridge. "Do you have any juice?" His voice is muffled.

When I come out of the bathroom, he's drinking a glass of water. "No. No juice."

He shrugs and goes back to the kitchen. I brush my teeth with a spanking-new toothbrush. I stand behind the bathroom door. Put on clothes from last night. This is tricky because I am technically still in my clothes from last night. It would be much nicer to grab some clean clothes, or at least some clean knickers. My clean clothes are back in my bedroom, in my dresser and in my drawers. But then I wouldn't have put on my clothes from last night. Quickly I take my clothes off. Then I put them back on again.

I don't brush my hair or wash my face or even have a glass of water.

When I come out of the bathroom, Seamus is standing beside my bed peering at my Cuisenaire rods.

"Are these rods? Like we used to have in school?"

"Yep. A relic from my childhood. Can't seem to part with them."

Then he picks up Nikola's photo.

"Is this your grandfather?"

He's holding it in both hands, so that it faces toward me. I walk toward him and take it out of his hands.

"No. No, he's not my grandfather. He's kind of . . . my hero."

"I'm guessing he's not a footballer."

"Nope."

"A dentist?"

"Ah, no."

I stand there, holding Nikola.

"Is he . . . coming to breakfast with us?"

I guess I've been holding him too long.

"No. He doesn't eat much."

"Then let's put him back and go. I'm starving."

I return Nikola to the bedside table. Facedown.

We walk. Down the hall, down the stairs, down the path. Along the street. We walk, and I do nothing from my old routine. We cross the street. This is so easy.

We don't speak as we walk because I am thinking of hands, and of the length of my fingers. The index finger on my left hand is 69 millimeters from the first crease to the tip, and my ring finger is 68.5 millimeters. The index finger on my right hand is 67

millimeters from the first crease to the tip, and my ring finger is also 67 millimeters.

Like every measurement ever taken, every measure of every single thing, these numbers are important. Digit ratio is the ratio of the length of your digits, from the first crease at the join of the hand to the tip. This is usually measured using the index and ring fingers, and differs between men and women. In men, the index finger is typically shorter than the ring finger; in fact, the index finger is only 96 percent as long as the ring finger. So an average digit ratio for a man is 0.96. In women, the fingers are either about the same length, or the index finger is slightly longer; a ratio of 1.00 or above. Mine, for example, are 1.007 on my left hand and 1.000 on my right.

I've read that the reason for this difference between the sexes is the effect of sex hormones on the fetus. When we are blobs in our mummies' tummies, we are exposed to different levels of sex hormones, especially testosterone and estrogen. Less testosterone and more estrogen, we remain little girls. Lots of testosterone and less estrogen and we become boys. And as well as growing penises, boys grow longer ring fingers.

So what? Well, testosterone has other effects and digit ratio is an excellent marker for these. So men with a lower ratio are more physically aggressive, have more

sperm and more babies, and are better at sports (and, surprisingly, music). Or so the theory goes. A man with a higher ratio would have a greater risk of heart disease, and more chance of being gay. Conversely, women with a high ratio (like me) are more fertile with a higher risk of breast cancer. If my ratio was lower, odds on I'd be more verbally aggressive, which I certainly don't need, and more likely to be a lesbian.

Things get interesting when you think about this in terms of evolutionary theory. We might know these differences are caused by testosterone, but why? Why did men evolve with a longer ring finger than women, when so many women I know seem evolutionarily predisposed to collect as many wedding, engagement, eternity and just plain ornamental rings as possible?

One theory is man's historical job: hunter and warrior. A longer ring finger confers more stability when spear throwing, either at a woolly mammoth or some other long-ring-fingered gentleman from another tribe. Hence the scarcity of female world darts champions. When you spend your day picking berries, cooking, and raising children, it really doesn't matter which finger is longest.

Or maybe it's got nothing to do with throwing spears. Maybe it's a result of selection, in other words maybe women subconsciously fancy men with a shorter

ratio. The sexual power of the appearance of a man's hands has long been underrated. Perhaps a woman's subliminal mind is thinking, "Sure, he's got a potbelly and a face that belongs on a wanted poster, but take a look at that ring finger."

Seamus Joseph O'Reilly has the sexiest hands I have ever seen. They are sometimes swaying at his sides, sometimes half in his pockets. At the café, he leans one against the door to open it for me. Inside I don't have to remember where I sat yesterday and sit at the next available table rotating in a clockwise direction. Seamus picks a table, chooses one that is somehow better than the others, and walks toward it. I don't have to decide anything. We both pick up menus.

When Cheryl sees us together, her smile fades. "Seamus? Company today?"

Hi, Cheryl. It's me, Grace. I come here every day. Remember?

"Good morning, Cheryl," Seamus says. "Special occasion." He gives me a sideways grin.

Cheryl squishes her face up like a piglet, pulls her notepad from her apron and waits.

"Grace?" Seamus says.

Breakfast. He wants me to order breakfast. The first thing on the menu under "Breakfasts" is "Fresh fruit with yogurt." But the first thing alphabetically is

"Bacon and eggs on toast." There are more headings, too: "Sides," "Coffee," "Tea," "Juices," "Smoothies." I should have a coffee: the first thing under "Coffee" is "Espresso." But then I should have the first thing under "Breakfasts," and the first side. But ordering fresh fruit with yogurt with bacon on the side sounds a wee bit stupid. Alphabetically, the first thing on the entire menu is "Apple juice." Perhaps I should have that.

They're waiting.

"You go."

"Berry and banana pancakes with maple syrup, thanks, Cheryl. And a cappuccino."

He's got to be kidding. Who eats that much sugar at this time of the morning? Does he know what that would do to his insulin levels? Those calories would feed a medium-size African village for a week.

They're still waiting.

I glance at Seamus, then back at the menu. "I'll have the same."

Cheryl writes, scowls and heads for the kitchen.

We're quiet for a moment. It is a comfortable silence, like we are both wondering if this will be the first of many breakfasts.

Still, there are things I have to know.

"So. Do you live around here?"

"Nope. Carnegie. I share a house with 2 of my brothers."

The coffees arrive. His perfect long fingers curl around his cup. The cup is nestled in his right hand, resting against the fleshy pad of his palm like he's holding a wineglass full of 1955 Grange. His left hand is over the top of his right, the fingers touching. I would give anything to measure those fingers right now, but I have no ruler or tape, and besides, I don't think it would look cool. Seamus sips happily, but I loathe coffee. To drink it I add 5 sugars. Together with the pancakes I should be in a diabetic coma by noon.

"What's that like, sharing with your brothers?"

"Shocking. They're animals. It's a temporary arrangement. One just broke up with his wife. The other is saving to go overseas. Soon I'll be rid of them. I love them, but God, this is too much."

The pancakes come, too fast. As I suspected: premade and heated in the microwave. A heart attack on a plate. Seamus eats like a starving man.

"2 brothers. No sisters?"

He raises his eyebrows. His mouth is full of pancake. He holds up 4 fingers and keeps chewing. "3 brothers," he says, "1 sister."

"5 of you? Wow. Pretty rare these days." I imagine 5 children playing hide-and-seek in an overgrown back-

yard. Climbing trees together. Backyard cricket, until one ball smashes the kitchen window and no one owns up. Running through the sprinkler in their underwear. Mum with a pitcher of cold orange cordial and 5 plastic cups. Dad teaching each one how to ride a bike. I take a bite. The maple syrup is imitation.

"Irish Catholics, remember? Either that, or the fact that my parents didn't own a TV until 1978. The old man thought it was a fad. 'I'm telling you, woman, they'll be stopping making these in 12 months, maybe less.'" He drains the last of his coffee then wipes the foam off his lip with his knuckle. "The day my mother made him buy one was the saddest day of his life."

"What number were you?" I lean forward, elbows on the table, chin resting on my hands.

"I am the second son. My brother Declan is the oldest. Then Dermot, Brian and Kylie. She's . . . a little slow. She still lives at home with Mum and Dad." He waves his empty cup in the air at Cheryl.

The café is starting to fill, smartly dressed women in designer jeans and peasant tops and beaded sandals. I don't care; I am following the plan and all those shriveled-up suburban women could only dream of having the night I had last night.

"So, Declan, Seamus, Dermot, Brian . . . and Kylie?"

He shrugs. "We were here by then. They wanted to fit in."

"Were you close together? In age, I mean."

His eyes narrow like he's trying to see something a long way away. "Close in both ways. Mum had 5 under 6, in a new country with no relatives, no friends and an accent that made her impossible to understand. Dad did his best, but he worked long hours and looking after children wasn't a man thing back then. And Kyles needed a bit of extra attention."

The 5 of them as toddlers, freshly bathed and wearing their jammies, sitting on the couch. Cuddled together smelling of baby powder and watching Disney on a Sunday night. Not like us, Jill and me. 2. Only 2. Each of us in our own room, me reading and Jill playing with dolls.

"Do you remember Ireland?"

"Not a thing. You'd think I would; I was 4 when we moved here. I went back in my early twenties expecting some kind of revelation. I guess you always romanticize, think what your alternative life would have been. I might as well have gone to Mars. It was fun but I felt no connection whatsoever."

"Possibly a bit late to ask this, but . . . single?"

He laughs. "Single, yes. Definitely single."

I wait.

"I was in a . . . relationship. We broke up last year."

"Why?"

He laughs again. " 'Why?' Jeez, Grace, don't hold back. If you want to know something, just come right out and ask."

I wait.

"Look . . . I like my life. I like my job, I like my house. I like going to football games and having friends around for a barbecue. On Sundays I go surfing with some mates. Ashleigh . . . she was into personal development courses and goal-setting and self-help books . . . She's going out with a property developer now. I hear they just bought a block of flats and a Subway franchise."

I scan his hazel eyes; they remain unclouded. No frown. The mouth does not purse, the way some do when discussing their exes.

"Date of birth?" His second coffee arrives. Cheryl takes my cappuccino away without asking. It is half drunk and cold, congealing on top.

"Into horoscopes, are you?" He scoops a piece of pancake on his fork using his knife, then a blueberry, then dips it in the maple-colored goo. He pops the little tower in his mouth. He doesn't bolt it down like some men. He chews and tastes. I've managed about 35 percent of 1 pancake. I'm still not hungry.

"Let's say I have an interest in numerology."

"Fifth of January." He wipes the corner of his mouth with a napkin, despite there being no food there.

Capricorn. He doesn't seem like an egomaniac. In my experience, Capricorns think they're Jesus Christ. Or else Jesus Christ thought he was the son of God because he was a Capricorn.

"1969, right?"

His fork freezes midway to his mouth. "How did you know that?"

Note to self: do not let new boyfriend think you are a stalker. I smile in a way I hope looks nonthreatening. "You told me last week in the café that you were 38. Remember?"

"Aah." Fork continues to mouth.

"What was your home address when you were little?"

"The house in Ireland I don't remember. I was 4 when we left. Here, it was 23 Carpenter Street, Vermont South."

Vermont South. I don't go that far on my holidays. I'll have to look it up.

At home in the bottom drawer of my bedside table I have a book that was a gift from my mother. It is a notebook with thin translucent pages and faint sky-blue lines. The cover is also blue, a heavy cloth that feels more like upholstery; a kind of a corduroy, but

with small, fine ridges. I always remember numbers, but I rarely store them. But now I will take out that book and write in it a list of numbers. Seamus numbers. I already have his phone number. I still need his current address, but I have 38, 5, 1, 1969, 4, 23. These I will begin with. Others, like the length of his index and ring fingers, and the number of ex-girlfriends, I will collect later.

"We came out for breakfast to talk about you and I've done all the talking. What was it you wanted to tell me?" He speaks like a man trying to coax a cat from a tree.

I look down at my plate. My breakfast is not muesli, low-fat yogurt and banana. My pancake is not surgically dissected into a predetermined number of bites. I am at the café and it's not 10:48 A.M.

"Nothing."

"What are you thinking about?"

I am thinking about numbers, of course, but also about those fingers, about where they could go and where I'd like them to go. And I'm thinking about all the clever women who choose men with long fingers.

"Egomaniac," I say. He blushes.

After breakfast, we walk back to the supermarket where he left his car. Old white Commodore. License

plate MDS 938. He kisses me, standing in the middle of the street. His kiss is less demanding than last night but more enticing. His stubble burns across my cheek. He gives me all his numbers and writes mine down on a tram ticket. I am listening hard, but he doesn't say "I'll call you."

Chapter 9

Now it's Sunday night. 8:00 P.M.

"Hello, Mother."

"Hello, dear. Have you had a nice week?"

"Dandy." Sex with a spunky Irishman on the kitchen floor. "How's Mr. Parker's rash?"

"Better, better. I read this horrible thing in the paper yesterday."

"Yes?"

"About these 2 boys, twins I think they were, 5 or 6 maybe, and anyway they didn't have a pet and they decided between themselves that they would play a game, that one would play at being the dog and the other would take the dog for a walk. So one of them, I can't remember which one, went into their parents' room and got this old belt of their father's

and before you know it he put it round his neck like a dog's collar and lead, you get it? Well you can imagine—choked his poor wee self, they couldn't get the belt off. It strangulated him. Horrible things they put in the paper these days, no regard for the feelings of the family. Makes me not want to read it anymore. What else do you think I could use for mulch, besides newspapers? Grace? Grace, are you still there?"

Still here. "Beats me. Junk mail? Magazines? Mr. Parker?"

"That's funny, dear. No, I'm sure the color of the ink wouldn't be good for the soil. Perhaps I'll keep buying the newspaper but not read it."

Then, 19 minutes later: "Hello, Gracie."

"Jill."

"Listen, I just wanted to let you know . . . I am going to China with Harry. The kids will be all right. Do you think the kids will be all right?"

"They'll be fine."

"They're each staying at a friend's place. So they'll go to school just like normal. And they're very mature for their age. So they'll be all right. And it's only for a week."

Yes, Jill. Everyone will be all right.

"And Mum will be okay. Do you think Mum will be okay?"

No, Jill. I think flesh-eating aliens will devour mother and pick their teeth with your children. I tell Jill I have to go. Can't talk. Busy thinking.

On Monday it's raining and 12 degrees. Unseasonable rain and unseasonable cold. I love Melbourne, but Jesus. It's the middle of summer and it's pelting down, each drop hard like ice. Hundreds and thousands of drops. Millions. Trillions. It throws me, the rain. It makes my breakfast seem stodgy and chilling to my bones. Breakfast is always 40.00 grams of untoasted muesli (the amount of fat in the toasted kind is unbelievable), 200.00 grams of low-fat yogurt (rotated from the left of the supermarket chilled cabinet and bought only in 5 sets of 2s—not the 6-packs, of course) and 1 banana, sliced into 10 chunks.

The rain makes me wish for toast soldiers dipped in boiled eggs.

Last year I bought a laboratory-grade scale. It's almost impossible to measure muesli to 2 decimal places. It's almost inhuman to eat the same food every day without variation. It's almost impossible to count your steps accurately in the rain because of an irresistible urge to avoid puddles.

I'm sick of this.

On Monday I didn't want to eat my breakfast. I nearly didn't go to the café, in favor of staying home

in front of the heater. Then I didn't feel like orange cake. The icing was drooping down the sides like it'd been sitting there all weekend. I had to force it down. 15 pieces. I didn't even touch the hot chocolate. When I got home I watched some old movie with Greer Garson on TV and did 10 sit-ups in one ad break then 10 squats in the next. I didn't feel like dinner either. The chopping and slicing seemed boring and pointless instead of rhythmic and calming. And chicken. Oh God, I'm so tired of chicken. I want to eat vegetable lasagna, puffed and browned and cheesy. I want to eat baked salmon sprinkled with lemon rind and capers and maybe a little dill, and potato gratin. Steak and kidney pie with a towering pastry crust 10 centimeters high that shatters against my fork. I want chili con carne with a hint of cumin that lingers, and tacos and bread and butter pudding and watermelon. Not together. Separately. I have eaten muesli, yogurt, banana, tuna and egg salad sandwich (alternating) and chicken and vegetables every single day since I stopped working. The same food for 24 months.

Monday night. No call.

On Tuesday the rain dips to showers. 18 degrees. I clean between the keys of my computer with a cotton bud dipped in tea tree oil, then call Larry. She's at a friend's house, Jill says. Jill reminds me, again, that she

is going to China. Jill does not ask if she can give the school my number as an emergency contact. Jill does not ask me to phone the kids to see how they are, or drop in on Mother or water the potted plants.

Tuesday night. No call.

I could ring him, you know. It's not the bloody 1950s. I'm not one of those game-playing women; I just can't decide when to call. Sunday night was obviously too soon. Monday night seemed a bit perfunctory, and Tuesday seemed like I had deliberately chosen Tuesday instead of Monday so as not to seem too keen. Then when he hadn't rung by Tuesday night I couldn't help wondering why. Perhaps he hated it. Perhaps I'm shocking in bed—too whorish. Not whorish enough? Sex too soon? Legs too hairy? Perhaps it's because we didn't have sex again in the morning. Perhaps that turned him off. Or perhaps he's one of those men who want the conquest, just once. Or perhaps he thinks I'm like that.

Wednesday. I rearrange my bookshelf, dissolving my alphabetical arrangement in favor of categories. Biographies first, then fiction then history then mathematics then medicine. Science last. Outside it's fine. 32. I clean the venetian blinds with hot soapy water and a sponge. 10 wipes on each blade. Wednesday night. No call. Thursday I scrub my skin with a loofah, 10

strokes each half limb. I exfoliate my face. 7 wrinkles around my left eye, 8 around my right. Not so long ago there were 6 around each. Would it be too much to ask for a little symmetry? The little bastards are breeding. Unlike me.

Perhaps I should do another proper spring clean, like my mother used to do. Although I've just done this; I spring clean twice a year, on the first of January for the new year and the first of September for the beginning of spring. Obviously it would be better if these 2 days were 6 months apart, but that can't be helped.

Despite the fact that I clean very differently from my mother—consciously so—there is something about my actions that reminds me of her. When I clean the house, every inch from the top of the picture rails to underneath the doors, I can close my eyes and be 9 years old. It was unbearably cold, as was every day in my memory's childhood, and my mother was fill-ing the incinerator and the warmth radiated in every direction. The smoke blew around the backyard like acid splashed in your face, toward the sheets waving on the clothesline, and I knew that when she took them down they would smell like smoke instead of air and she would wash them again. Yet she didn't move them or wait until the burning was over before hanging them on the line. Small bits of paper—fragments of color-ing books, pieces of butcher paper—and even threads

from clothing blew around the mango tree in an eddy. I poked in the ashes with a stick to find discolored lumps of plastic and charred metal, pieces of GI Joe dolls and a train set.

Inside the house everything changed from a solid to a liquid. Instead of being in its place and dry, everything—furniture, cushions, curtains—flowed from room to room and place to place as she scrubbed floors and let them dry, and everything was wet. She had Jill and me pull sheets and old medicines and jumpers and the plastic Christmas tree out of closets. Even the tiny space where we kept the linen napkins we never used was cleared; my thin arm would snake into every corner where Jill's chubbier one couldn't reach. All the sheets and blankets were washed and hung, dripping and heavy, on the line. Bathroom cabinets were emptied, each tube and box checked. Kitchen drawers were upturned, washed and fitted with fresh paper. All the Tupperware was soaked and scrubbed and sunned. Armed with a bucket and sponge, Jill and I scoured the fly screens that my mother had removed from the high windows while teetering on the kitchen stool. She used the same stool to wash the light fittings, slopping soapy water as she went.

This went on from dawn, and all day we ate only apples since they needed neither cutlery nor plates. Eventually, late into the night, naked since all our

clothes were still drying, Mother would mop the floor starting from the farthest corner and ending at her bed, into which we 3 would collapse and sleep without sheets or pillowcases. My father had some precognition of Mother's cleaning spells, like a farm animal sensing the coming of a storm. The day before she began, his car would fill with his fishing gear and a tent. If I'd been asked at the time I would have said he'd gone camping with friends. Now I'm equally sure he went alone.

Even as a child I guessed there was something my mother was desperate to wash away, something that needed to be burned or rinsed or scrubbed at any cost. She was blind to the fact that nothing needed cleaning because these attacks were so frequent, yet there was order and safe structure in her work. That energy is gone now from my mother and all that remains is the way she speaks continuously without breathing or thinking. As a child I would sit up at night to make her gifts—a photo frame edged with seashells, a fired coffee mug I bought blank then painted. Once I embroidered "mother" on a pillowcase in cursive pink script. I made these things to see the care on her face when she polished or laundered them.

I don't clean that way. I divide the tasks into smaller jobs, writing them down on a small pad.

1. Remove articles from desk, 10 things at a time.

2. Dust desk.

3. Spray and polish desk.

4. Replace articles on desk, 10 things at a time.

The best way is to break this up so that the steps are quite discrete—either by reading 10 pages of a book, then doing a step, then reading another 10 pages, or rotating the rooms. Usually I love it but this week even cleaning is beyond me, except the venetians. I couldn't figure out where or when to start.

Thursday afternoon, fine, 36 degrees. 3:40 P.M. The phone rings.

For a minute I stare at it. Either Mother is dead, or it's Seamus.

"Hello?"

"Um . . . hello, Grace? It's Seamus."

"Seamus, Seamus . . . Oh, I remember. Kitchen-floor Seamus."

"As opposed to whom? Driveway Seamus? Kitchen-countertop Seamus? You're not making me feel special, Grace."

"Not my problem. There's a veritable St. Patrick's Day parade of Seamuses over here."

"I see. Well, is there any way I can improve my standing among your Seamuses?"

"I'm listening."

"Just a sec." He gets a bit blurry. *"Mate, we don't show those kind of films. Nope. Nothing with talking fish or cars or rats. It's an anthropomorphization-free zone. Try the multiplex at the top of Swanston Street."*

"You're at work?"

"Yeah. It's dead here today. It's a shame. We all thought this Paul Cox retrospective would be huge."

"Imagine. Parents preferring talking fish to voyeurism and leprosy."

"Exactly. Just a sec." More mumbles. *"Mate, you go to any cinema in town and they all charge that. It doesn't go into my pocket. Well, you don't have to buy it. You could bring a sandwich from home."*

"You tell him. A small Coke should cost $38."

"You'd be great in here. Any time you're looking for a job . . ."

"Thanks, but I've been flat-out cleaning today. In my French maid's outfit and high heels."

"Let's stop right there," he says. "Are you free Sunday, around 11?"

"I can be."

"Good. I'll pick you up."

"Where are we going?"

"Chinese."

Chapter 10

It's Sunday, 24 degrees. It's 10:30 A.M. but I'm ready, because this is my usual going-out time. I'm wearing a black cotton knitted shirt and an olive-green peasant-style skirt with drawstring waist. And black-heeled sandals. In my mind I've substituted "go for Chinese" for "walk to café." I'm even prepared to visualize the whole café experience—walk, ordering, orange cake—while I'm at the restaurant.

When I open the door, Seamus Joseph O'Reilly is standing there. Hawaiian shirt, pale blue jeans. Deck shoes. (I'm picking up a distinct eighties theme.) He looks gorgeous. He even smells gorgeous. I'm tempted to forget about going out and invite him inside, even though it's now past my going-out time. But he kisses my cheek in a perfunctory way, and before I know it we're in MDS 938, and we're off.

The restaurant is overwhelming: tables, people, carts. Wall hangings. Children running around. So many things to count. I take my mind off it by thinking about being Chinese. I love Chinese everything. Fireworks, noodles. The Wall. I love the way they don't compartmentalize their numbers but integrate them into daily life. I like the way that zero is the most complex pictogram of all the single digits. A big fat 0 like we use doesn't sum up the magnitude of the concept.

I love lucky numbers. In Chinese culture they're 6, 8 and 9. The reason they're considered lucky is probably the sound that they make. 6 sounds like the word for "everything going smoothly," *liu*. 8 sounds like *fa*, which means "great fortune coming soon." And 9 sounds like *jiu*, the word for "everlasting," especially when used about a marriage or a friendship. I remember reading about some Hong Kong millionaire who paid a fortune for a license plate beginning with 888. These plates become a circular argument: everyone knows how expensive they are, so they treat you with more respect. And the more people bow down to you, the luckier (and richer) you get.

Is it true that Monterey Park in the United States has the nation's highest concentration of Chinese, because the area code was originally 818? That no Chinese

would live in a house numbered 14 because it means instant death?

Sitting in the restaurant, looking at the silver trolley covered with little bamboo steamers, I'm feeling very unlucky indeed. I probably need to get a shirt with an 8 on it. He's done the gentlemanly thing all morning and now he's waiting for me to choose. And I know I should. I need a system. A pattern. I'll even eat the chicken feet if it's called for.

But I'm defeated. Too many carts, too many steamers. "What should I try?"

He leans closer and points to a few dishes with his chopsticks. The smiling waitress puts three steamers on our table. He doesn't smile back. Instead he looks down and stabs at a green dumpling. Prawn and chive, I think. He eats it. 2 bites.

A waitress arrives with a white pot in each hand. "Tea?"

What, no drinks menu? What other choices are there? How can I decide just like that?

"Grace? Do you want some tea?"

"Do I?"

"Yes," he says, a little too firmly. "Yes, tea. For both of us."

The waitress pours the tea. When do I sip? Now? Or should I alternate between bites of the dumpling?

Actually, how many bites in one dumpling? 10 would be ridiculously small. Even 5 wouldn't look right. Seamus had 2 before, but his mouth is probably bigger than mine.

"So . . . I hope I didn't catch you in the middle of anything when I phoned on Thursday."

"No, no. A spot of nuclear fission in the kitchen, that's all."

"You're not . . . working at the moment?"

"No. Not . . . at the moment."

"Haven't found the right job? Or taking a break?"

I don't answer. I can't answer. I can see where this is going. Oh God. I shouldn't have come.

"Don't you like Chinese food?"

"Um . . . yes. It all looks so good. I can't decide what to have first."

I sit silently for another moment while he stabs another dumpling. But he doesn't eat it. He lays the skewered dumpling down on his plate.

"Grace, we need to talk." Why is it that when men have something on their minds, they revert to clichés?

"Hang on, I'm the chick. That's supposed to be my line." He lays his chopsticks down flat on the table. His nostrils flare out, and he takes a deep breath and lets it out.

Under the table, I ball my hands into fists.

"I really like you, Grace. I really do. You're funny and sexy and . . . great. You're great." He pauses and sips his tea.

Oh God. I should have known. Men love to dump you in public places so you won't make a scene, and there's nowhere more public than this.

"Can I ask a personal question?"

"Yes, I've always been a woman. I should probably wax more often." I absolutely refuse to get upset. I refuse to let a man I've known for 22 days hold that kind of power.

He doesn't smile. I try again.

"Never before, I promise. You were the first."

Nothing.

"Only once, but I didn't inhale?"

Tough audience.

"Grace, can you stop joking for a minute? I want to know what's going on with you." The crinkles around his eyes turn into furrows. He sucks on his bottom lip.

I can feel a blush coming up my neck and across my face. "I don't know what you mean." I look down. He has chosen one steamer of prawn dumplings, one of wontons and one with a radish cake. The bamboo steamers are in a circle and because there is no beginning and no end I don't know where to begin. Usually in this situation I try to picture a clock and choose

whatever is just past noon but the radish cake is kind of in the middle and I can't work that into the scheme. Instead I sip my tea.

"Look, I know this is none of my business, Grace, but . . . Why did you take that banana at the supermarket? You had lots of bananas already."

I don't say anything. I can't.

"Grace? When we hold hands, your fingers twitch. When we walk, your lips move."

"I didn't realize about my fingers. It's only a habit. If you had told me when I was doing it I could have stopped it."

His voice drops to near a whisper and he leans forward. "It's not just that. Why don't you order your own food? Even now you haven't eaten anything—you didn't even know if you wanted tea. And why haven't you got a job? You're obviously intelligent and capable. What's going on?"

I close my eyes for a moment. I'm not worried. I refuse to be worried.

He leans back in his chair. "God . . . look, you don't have to answer. Okay? Forget it."

The excited chatting of the restaurant has settled into a background hum. At the table next to us 5 people sit with 10 chopsticks in their 5 hands. They have 14 bamboo steamers, which seems ridiculous because that

is 2.8 steamers each and by the time they work their way around some dumplings will be cold. Why would people order like that? There are 4 carts after all and they come around every couple of minutes—too often in fact. How do they expect you to eat when you have to say "no, thank you" every 2 minutes? Each cart has 7 rows of steamers; on the one nearest us the first 4 rows from the front have 4 steamers across, the fifth row has 3 and the last 2 rows have 4. Some are 3 high, some are 5 high, some are singles. The cart nearest us has 87 steamers; the other carts are hidden behind diners and I can't be sure how many they have. Still, there's no excuse for 14 on 1 table. Even if there is only 1 left of something you really like, say the oysters with the cheese sauce on top, you can always ask them to make more.

"Is that really important?" I say. "Is it really important that I don't have a job?"

"Maybe not. Maybe it's not important. But fuck it, Grace, I looked in your fridge last Sunday morning. What's with all the plastic bags full of stuff? I've never seen a fridge where nothing—I mean nothing—is in its original packaging. A fridge full of bags of onions and beans and God knows what else all in little individual Ziploc bags. Yogurt, even. And all your drinking glasses have lines drawn across them, like glasses in wine bars."

I think he's finished, but he's just warming up. "You don't even have a roll of toilet paper, just a pile of lengths already ripped. There's a ruler next to your dental floss and there's a little measuring cup in the shower next to the shampoo. God, I've never seen so many clocks in my life. It's like a clock store. And let's not forget the toothbrushes. Why on earth would anyone buy 17 toothbrushes?"

All of a sudden the room is quiet. The tea has spilled because of that sloppy way they pour it in Chinese restaurants and there are 3 stains on the tablecloth: the first quite small, the second bigger and the third an irregular middle-size splodge in the shape of Tasmania. There are 3 prawn dumplings going cold. Why do they serve them in 3s? 3s is probably the most inconvenient serving size possible. How often do 3 people go out together for brunch? 2, yes. 4, yes. But 3? Perhaps they know you can't split them evenly so you're forced to get another steamer, the way small packets of potato chips are a tiny bit too small to satisfy but the big ones are just a bit too much. Another minor evil of the capitalist system. The prawn dumplings have 12 little twists along the top of the dough, probably made by hand.

"Grace? Shit, I'm sorry. Really. Come on. We don't have to talk about it."

"14," I say.

He looks at me blankly.

"I bought 14 toothbrushes." I take my second sip of tea.

Then I feel a twinge in my stomach. It can't be the food because I haven't eaten anything yet. It's not that I'm frightened of serious conversations. Not long before the execution of Kemmler, Nikola and Westinghouse had a very important conversation about a deal. The kind of conversation that had been brewing for a while and was painful while it happened, but ultimately for the best.

Nausea flows through me like a wave, starting in my mouth and sweeping down my torso. I'm definitely sick, very sick.

"Grace? Are you okay?"

Possibly I look a little pale.

"I . . . I don't feel very well." Possibly I'm going to vomit all over the cute little bamboo baskets.

"Do you need some air?"

I don't reply.

"Would you like to go outside?"

I nod, holding my stomach. My mouth tastes of acid.

Seamus looks at the bill and leaves some notes on the table. He takes my arm. I can barely keep my feet as we walk to the door. You see, the problem with the deal

was this: Westinghouse offered Nikola a royalty payment of $2.50 per horsepower of electricity sold. Even the great Westinghouse did not foresee exactly how generous this was and exactly how much horsepower he was going to sell.

Across the street there's a park; we sit on the swings. I am doubled over in pain. It's unlikely to be appendicitis because that would begin with constipation and some general, low-level gut ache. Could be some kind of inflammatory bowel disease, but then I'd have diarrhea. It's probably not an aortic aneurism. Although it could be. Maybe it's last night's chicken, or it's a virus and I'll be over it in a day or so.

Seamus is kneeling beside the swing, frowning. He wants to know about me. He wants to know who I am.

Eventually Westinghouse was drowning in debt. So he went to Nikola and said, simply and plainly, "Nik, mate. We're in a bit of trouble. Mind if, instead of $2.50 per horsepower, I pay you nothing?"

I made this bit up.

If this had happened today with a lesser man, it's easy to see what would happen. Lawyers. Litigation. You read about the smallness of people every day: people who blame the city council when their car hits a traffic light when they are driving drunk. People who sue restaurants for not warning them that coffee is hot.

This packet of nuts may contain traces of nuts. People who can't accept that it's their own fault.

It is, you know. It's all your own fault, everything, everything, everything.

Nikola was not small. His reply was recorded and is probably the most beautiful speech ever uttered. Above anything it shows the intrinsic goodness of the man.

"Mr. Westinghouse," Nikola said, "you have been my friend, you believed in me when others had no faith; you were brave enough to go ahead when others lacked courage; you supported me when even your own engineers lacked vision to see the big things ahead that you and I saw; you have stood by me as a friend; you will save your company so that you can develop my inventions. Here is your contract and here is my contract—I will tear both of them to pieces, and you will no longer have any troubles from my royalties. Is this sufficient?"

"I want to help you, Grace. I do. If it's a religious thing where you can't drive or use a mobile phone or if it's a food allergy thing . . . I need to know what I'm getting into."

This man I've met 4 times is kneeling at my feet. His hand is on my knee. He has not spoken about the weather. He has not spoken about football. Against

every social instinct he has spoken from his heart. Most people say, "Too much information." Not Seamus.

"Grace?" He sits on the swing next to mine. He's waiting.

If I told Nikola, I know what he would say. He would say "Grace, you have been my lover. Tell me your troubles, and I will tear them to pieces, and you will no longer have any troubles. Is this sufficient?"

I take a deep breath.

"It's not a religion. It's nothing like that. It's just that I like to count things. I need to count things," I say, digging the toes of my shoes into the pulverized rubber below the swings.

"Count things? Like what?"

"Like steps and syllables and bites and things. Food. Brushes of my hair. Brushes of my teeth."

He's frowning. Fuck it. Keep going.

"Volume of shampoo. Number of beans for dinner. Bananas. Number of items in a load of washing. I make lists of the number of dishes I wash and the surfaces I've dusted to make sure I don't lose count. I check the time a lot. You know. Things."

"Like those people who wash their hands all day? Obsessive-compulsive, is that what they call it?"

I snort. "Christ no. Nothing like those crazy hand-washers. There are 182 different species of bacteria on

the human skin. They're all there for a reason. Trying to scrub them away is illogical."

"And counting is . . . logical?"

"Of course. Counting is what defines us. Listen, Seamus . . . the only thing that gives our lives meaning is the knowledge that eventually we will all die. All of us. That's what makes each minute important. Without the ability to count our days, our hours, our loved ones . . . there's no meaning. Our lives would have no meaning. Without counting, our lives are unexamined. Not valued. Not precious. This consciousness, this ability to rejoice when we gain something and grieve when we lose something—this is what separates us from other animals. Counting, adding, measuring, timing. It's what makes us human."

"I see. I . . . hadn't thought of it like that. This explains the rods."

My rods. I wish I had them with me right now, just to hold in my pocket. I try to smile. "My most prized possession. If my flat was on fire, the rods would be the only thing I'd grab. I spend hours playing with them."

In about 10 minutes he'll leave and I'll never see him again. I look over to where he's sitting and focus. I need to memorize everything—the way his limbs arrange themselves on the swing. The silhouette of his head against the trees. His Hawaiian shirt is bright

yellow flowers on a black background; I can count 8 whole flowers from here, plus 15 part flowers. His jeans are worn to white on the left knee. The exact timbre of his voice. I shut my eyes for a second to see if I can re-create him.

"So why don't you have a job?"

"The school had some weird idea that I was paid to teach children, not count them. As a rule employers don't approve of you counting instead of working. Un-reasonable, I know. Also I can't drive anymore. Spend-ing the entire time staring at the speedometer to make sure it's exactly on the limit—kind of dangerous."

For a while he swings, tipping his head back to look at the sky. His arms are stretched out and his feet are extended, like a small boy with his father behind him, pushing.

"What does your family say?"

"Mum and Jill? They know, obviously. They know I can't work, and once . . . well, I went to the hospital once and they came to see me. Jill is annoyingly under-standing. Mother is afraid it was something she did, so she doesn't want to know. Larry, that's Jill's middle child . . . she just accepts it. As if I had double-jointed elbows or could bend my thumb back to reach my wrist. I don't care what anybody else thinks."

"Have you seen anyone about it? Someone profes-sional, I mean." He turns and looks at me. The sun is

behind me, and both eyes crinkle and one closes be-
cause he can't shield them while he's swinging.

"A therapist. I had kind of a bad turn; that was when
I stopped going to work. I saw a therapist, twice a week,
for a while. She wanted me to take antidepressants. We
did hypnotism, the whole bit. She was younger than
me—possibly she was about 12. Every appointment
made her more irritated, like I was still counting simply
to spite her. I felt like taking her out for an ice cream to
apologize."

"What did she say was behind it?" He's stopped
swinging now. He stands up and kneels on the swing.

"It doesn't matter. It doesn't matter what she said.
She took one little event from my childhood and blew
it right out of proportion because of some archaic
Freudian perspective that says everything has one
simple cause."

He leaves his swing and walks over to mine. I'm
panicked for a moment. What is he doing? I won't be
able to bear it if he holds my hand and looks into my
eyes, all sympathy. If he tries to unravel me. If he kneels
beside me and touches my knee like I've got cancer,
I'll scream. If he looks at me with that mix of concern
and relief—the furrowing of his brow meant to be em-
pathetic but that really conveys triumph, because no
matter how fucked-up his life might be, it isn't as bad
as mine—well, if he does that, I won't cope at all. If he

looks at me like that, so help me, I'll punch him right
in the face.

But he doesn't. He doesn't touch me. Instead he
stands behind my swing and gives it a push. I shut my
eyes as I feel the breeze on my face and in my hair.

"Humor me," he says.

Not this again. Jesus. Move on. Move on.

"When I was little something happened. It's a small,
very small incident that I've dealt with so many times.
It was very upsetting, I'll admit, but kids will be kids,
and I refuse to bow down to it. I refuse to blame who I
am, and I kind of like who I am by the way, on one in-
cident, one minute out of a lifetime of minutes. Besides,
I don't have a problem with it. I can discuss it anytime.
The fact is that they don't know why I'm like I am;
they have no bloody idea. It's easier to pin it on one
thing than to think about the complexity of an entire
person."

"So tell me." I can't see him. I'm only conscious of
those hands pushing me.

I shut my eyes. Even on this warm day the chain is
cold to the touch; it must leave blisters on smaller, softer
hands. Tell him the truth. Be big, like Nikola. Then he
will know the heart of you, and if he decides to leave
then you have the diamond-clear and sharp knowledge
that, for a moment at least, he knew you.

Chapter 11

The swing creaks, once on the upswing and once on the downswing. Tired wooden plank attached to a chain. The sky-blue paint on the chain has peeled from years of exposure to sun and rain, and with each movement of the swing a fine red dust floats to the ground.

"My parents were very proud of me," I hear myself say. "I was bright at school. So grown-up. They bragged about me constantly to their friends and relatives. Showed everyone my report cards. As a special treat, because I was so mature, when I was 8 we were given a puppy for Christmas. It was a soft, adorable little bundle of mischief. People didn't train their dogs so much in those days. Puppies were just puppies until they got older and learned better. Anyway this puppy was just plain annoying. For some reason it didn't take

to Jill the way it did to me. It followed me everywhere. I was supposed to look after it. I was the big girl."

I could see the backyard from my room. Our house was long and narrow, a single-fronted double-story terrace. In the middle of the yard, at the end of the concrete path, was the incinerator. In the right corner was an enormous flowering gum tree, and in front of that was the clothesline. I can see it now, easily, without even shutting my eyes because my whole mind back then was turned to escaping.

"Mum and Dad worked so hard to buy the place— nice house, nice suburb—so that their kids would have a better start than they did. Down the back was this steep set of steps. The puppy was so small. Couldn't possibly negotiate all those stairs by himself. My mother told me over and over: 'If you go out the back door, be sure and shut it so the puppy doesn't fall down the stairs.'"

"Oh God," Seamus says.

"One day I forgot. He fell down the back stairs." I look up to the sky, a moment of silent prayer, but I'm not sure he notices. "The puppy died."

"You poor little thing. You must have been devastated."

Poor little thing. Tell him. Tell him everything. Everything.

With my eyes closed I can gauge the movement of the swing as it arcs back to meet his hands. I can feel his hands go back with the swing just a little before he leans toward it and pushes it forward. I imagine his legs astride, the left slightly ahead of the right. Any deviation in the pace or the effort or the speed will reflect hesitation in his mind, and I will have lost him. I am alert for the movement of the swing to change, but it doesn't. It continues, up and down, like we are discussing the chances of rain.

"He just tumbled down. Hit his head. Died instantly without even a whimper. He lay at the bottom of the stairs like he was sleeping. This is the worst part: seeing him there, lying dead like that, my only thought was for myself. That my parents would no longer think me wonderful."

"What was his name?"

"Rusty," I say. "His name was Rusty."

That's it. That's as far as I can go. I can't do more than that.

Seamus gives the swing another push. "How did your parents react?"

"They were distraught. I mean, they didn't blame me, they really didn't. And they had owned dogs before. Puppies die, you know, they get hit by cars and God knows what. I suppose it was the shock that it

might have been one of us, Jill or me, who could have fallen. And because it was an accident they saw it as repudiation. That they weren't good enough parents."

The street is quiet. No more late arrivals, and the early diners are leaving. I stretch out my leg, hold it straight against the pressure of the air rushing toward me.

"The old guy in the photo?"

"Nikola Tesla. Inventor. Born 1856. Mad about counting. Counted everything."

"Tesla? As in Tesla coil?"

My shoulders drop. I hadn't realized they were tensed. Seamus has heard of Nikola. Billions haven't, but Seamus has. My stomach feels better. I should carry antacid with me but there are 14 tablets in a roll and that gives me the creeps.

"At high school we all had to write projects on famous inventors. Alexander Graham Bell, Fleming. You know. I'd never heard of Nik—Tesla before. I thought I was the only person in the world with this thing for counting. A bit of a freak, I guess. As a teenager I could easily have . . . sometimes I felt it would be better for everyone if I wasn't around. When I read about him, found out that someone as great as Tesla was also a counter . . . It just about saved my life."

"So . . . this accident . . . do you think it's behind your . . ."

He hesitates for a second and for an instant I think he's going to say "sickness."

I reach out my foot and dig it into the rubber. He stops pushing and I swing to a stop.

"No. No, I don't. I don't go into spasms if I see a puppy. I don't cower in the corner at the sight of stairs. I can talk about it very easily. People have much worse trauma than that. Besides, I've done my penance."

I can feel the warmth of the sun on my face. I walk around the swing and stand in front of him. I lift my arms and slide them up his shirt, around his neck, and nestle my fingers in the short hairs at the nape. He brings his hands to my hips and hooks his thumbs inside my waistband.

"And what penance is that?"

"I made a pledge to be very, very nice to animals." I nibble his Adam's apple.

He pulls me closer and gestures back at the restaurant. "You didn't eat a thing in there. Once again I've failed to feed you."

"Never mind," I say. "You can make it up to me somehow."

The drive home is too long. Red lights. A Volvo in front of us. The block of flats has too many stairs, 10 times as many as it did this morning. I fumble with the key even though I have opened this door 10,000

times. The door takes too long to open because the hinges are in slow motion. Inside, there's no hope of reaching the bedroom. It's miles away.

Seamus kicks the door closed with one leg and pushes me against the hallway wall. His open mouth is on my throat, but he can only kiss one hollow at a time. I can't undo his belt fast enough. Can't pull his shirt over his head because his hands are lifting up my skirt.

One arm is tight around my waist, the other yanks my underpants down. His trousers are already on the floor around his ankles. He lifts me and rams my inner thigh—the angle is all wrong. My underpants are caught around my knees, too high for my legs to spread.

"Fuck," he mutters. This time he rips my underpants all the way down. They pool on the floor.

Later I'll take my time. I'll feel the taut skin of his cock in my hand and in my mouth. I'll tongue him and he'll feel my hard teeth and my soft lips and I'll suck him hard and soft just to hear him moan. Later he'll be under me, and how deep, how fast, how long will all be up to me.

But not now. Now I can't wait, not one more second. His hands are big and wide on the cheeks of my bottom. He spreads them apart and lifts me again. The wall is hard against the small of my back and it pinches my hair.

For an instant, we don't move. Then I sink down on him and wrap my legs around his waist. I claw his back. He clenches his teeth and puts one hand on the wall to brace himself. He is inside me. It's exquisite . . . if I lean forward . . .

But then he stops, and shudders. I can feel the spasms inside me. His strength seems to drain and he leans against me. I unwrap my legs; they take my weight with only a little wobble. We rest, standing together, both sweating.

"Shit . . . I'm sorry." His breathing is heavy. "That was—"

"It's okay." I hope I sound convincing.

"Perhaps we should try it in a bed sometime."

"Good idea," I say. "How about now?"

In the afternoon we sleep together in my single bed. At least Seamus does. I can't. I can only look at him. As soon as Seamus closed his eyes, I turned Nikola facedown.

Nikola, like all truly great people, had a truly great obsession. People don't understand obsessions. An obsession is not a weakness. An obsession is what lifts people up, what makes them different from the gray masses. Do you think we'd still be talking about Romeo and Juliet today, over four hundred years since its first performance, if the two lovebirds had followed

their parents' advice and each settled down with more appropriate partners in four-bedroom, two-and-a-half-bathroom neo-Georgians in a new subdivision on the outskirts of Verona?

Nikola once misjudged the electricity coming from one of his machines and 3.5 million volts went through his body, leaving a mark on his chest on entry and a burned heel on exit. Another time he was experimenting with an oscillator, a device used to amplify mechanical vibrations. It caused a mini-earthquake, shattering windows all over Manhattan, and confirmed his belief that, with a little experimentation to find the exact frequency, he'd be able to split the earth in half like an apple. He loved talking about Martians. He wasn't a popular guy. He left New York in a hurry and moved to Colorado Springs, and that was the beginning of his obsession.

My obsession leaves at 5:12 P.M., after kissing me for 8 minutes at the top of the stairs.

I can't get Seamus Joseph O'Reilly out of my head. My routine becomes mechanical, the counting without any pleasure or purpose. I speak to him every night; who phones whom no longer seems important. Tuesday and Wednesday he visits late at night and stays until dawn.

I think of him every second. I cook my food but can't eat it. I can't sleep much, and when I do I dream of arms around my breasts, dreams so clear that it takes a few moments on waking to realize he isn't there.

On Thursday night when the phone rings, I jump.

"I'm so sorry it's not a Sunday," Jill says.

"It's okay." This new sexy me is almost adaptable.

"Harry and I leave for China tomorrow—"

"I think you may have already mentioned that."

"Hilly has a violin recital on Saturday. I discussed it with her weeks ago, and she said it was okay that we would be overseas. But this morning she made a fuss about it. I think she's upset that no one in the family will be there."

"Relevance to me?"

"Look, Grace, I know it's hard for you. But is there any chance you could be there?"

She interprets my silence as reluctance.

"It's the school fair—there'll be stalls and things. I've been making jams for weeks. Hilly can get there by herself—she's staying over at Stephanie's place. Stephanie plays the cello. You could meet her there. I don't want her to be the only girl with no family in the audience."

I'm distracted for a moment by a vision of Seamus as a schoolboy. I doubt he was the violin type. Not

the chess type, either. I'm thinking tennis. Or cricket. Imagine a little boy with Seamus's eyes, bat in hand, concentrating. My heart squeezes. I'd like to see Larry play her violin, but how? Before I can stop myself, it's out of my mouth.

"I'll get Seamus to take me."

There's silence for a moment, and for a moment I think I'm safe; she's distracted by a burglar or perhaps a fire in the kitchen.

"Who's Seamus?"

"He's a friend."

"A friend? You mean a boyfriend? You're seeing somebody?"

"A little less astonishment would be flattering, Jill."

"Gracie, darling . . . it's not that. You're beautiful, and so clever. It's just . . . do you think you're ready?"

"We've been out a few times, that's all. No vows exchanged."

"Do we get to meet him?"

"Yes . . . Maybe . . . I don't know. Let's see how it goes at the recital."

"Hilly would love to be the first one to meet him. Do you think . . . ? Do you think you'll be okay?"

I'm a new woman with a new boyfriend. Everything is peachy.

"Yes."

When I hang up from Jill I start to dial Seamus's number. Then I hang up again. Possibly this is not such a good idea. Possibly it is too soon to invite him to my niece's recital; too family-ish, too connected. But new women are brave, so I do ring and I ask him. He is surprised and delighted. He says yes.

On Saturday morning I wake as the alarm goes off at 5:55 A.M., alone, panting and sweating. I stare at my clock. The word "digital" comes from digits. How could I have forgotten this? I've been counting things in my mind, but not with my hands. I don't really know how many books I have, or spoons or hairpins. I feel dizzy and there is a pain in my chest that radiates down my left arm. The 5 digits of my left hand are tingly. All this time I've never thought about it. What if the answers are different? What if the numbers that come from minds are different from the numbers that come from hands? It's our digits that dictate the numbers, not obscure processes in our minds that can't even be seen. My heart has 4 chambers and a myriad of tiny blood vessels serving each one. What if one of those blood vessels isn't right? I remember reading somewhere about a man who was only 36; he had a congenital kink in one of his coronary arteries. He wasn't overweight. He was skinny, if I remember

rightly, and didn't smoke or drink. One day he was chopping wood in the backyard and felt kind of sick. He told his wife he didn't feel well so he went to bed early. She rushed him to the hospital in the middle of the night for a bypass. No one would have guessed. No warning signs. How many pieces of wood did he chop? And if he'd chopped fewer, would it have made a difference?

If I don't find out what I own, I'm going to die.

I stumble out of bed. To my left is the bedside table, and on top is my notepad and pen. It's enough to make categories now. Later I'll alphabetize them and type them on the computer. But I must count everything with my hands. Now. This is the only way I can save myself. Half-empty bottles of vitamins, 1, 2. My fingers jerk downward, marking off each item, crashing into my palm. Articles torn from magazines on counting, 1, 2, 3, 4. Christmas cards from last year, including those from the real estate agent and local pizzeria, neither of which I frequent, 1, 2, 3, 4, 5, 6, 7.

I drop to my knees and start on my chest of drawers, then rush back to the bedside table like I've been slapped. 2 half-empty bottles of vitamins, but how many pills in each? 8 in one, 14 in the other. Back to the chest of drawers. Start from the top left drawer and work across and down, like reading. The labels on the inside of each drawer that define the contents are a

further slap. They should have the number of items as well. Stupid, stupid girl. Undies, pajamas, swimsuits, socks, T-shirts, shorts, tracksuits, trousers, jumpers, thermals, sarongs, cardigans. Make piles. Count each one using my hands. Write the number in the book and on the label. Put everything back. Move on to wardrobe. When I go faster I feel the pain in my chest lessen. If I stop and breathe it comes back worse. I can see the narrow spot where the stent will eventually go, so narrow that each red blood cell is barely able to squeeze past. Faster, faster.

Finally the bedroom is finished, and so is the bathroom. Everything counted on my hands, everything written down in my book. I am halfway through the kitchen when the doorbell rings. At first I ignore it. It must be Jehovah's Witnesses or something. Who else would ring someone's doorbell at this time of the morning? I've a good mind to tell them to leave me alone to worship in peace at the feet of Satan, and by the way, remember 2 Samuel 22:28. That being, You save the humble but Your eyes are on the haughty to bring them low.

Then I glance at the clock. It's 11:52. Almost time to leave for the recital. It's Seamus at the door.

I'm still in my pajamas. I haven't showered or brushed my teeth or had breakfast or been to the café. The contents of the kitchen cupboards are all over the

floor. My notepad is filled with pages of tables, lines drawn and crossed through, and numbers. My right hand is sore and stiff.

I will have to explain it to him. I'm busy and I can't come. This has to be done; I simply can't live in a world if I don't know its dimensions. Each breath makes my chest ache and the pain radiates down my arm and across my back. I'll explain to him that, although I've obviously counted everything before, the word "digital" comes from the fingers. It's incomplete unless I count with my fingers. That's all there is to it. I open the door.

"You're not ready," he says. He doesn't sound surprised.

I lean in and close the door behind me so the kitchen chaos isn't so apparent. "I'm not feeling very well. I'll call Larry later and explain."

Gently he moves me out of the way and comes inside. Every plate and cup and sponge and vegetable peeler from every kitchen cupboard is piled on the countertops and on the floor. 2 frying pans are balancing on the 3 saucepans and the 5 little nested plastic cup measures have rolled into the hallway. One salad bowl holds the 10 knives, the other the 10 forks. The 10 spoons are in the strainer. The wineglasses, 2 sizes, 10 each, are on the kitchen counter, together with 9 champagne flutes.

The remaining champagne flute is on the scales, because while I'm counting I'm also checking what everything weighs. Might save time later. Every door is open, the labels on the inside of each door clearly visible. Next to each label I've attached a piece of string tied to a pen with sticky tape, like they do at the bank. (I buy my pens in boxes of 100.) So if I take a plate out to make a sandwich for lunch, I can easily adjust the total number of plates down. And when I replace it after it's been washed I can easily adjust the total number of plates up.

It looks worse than it is.

He stands still for a moment. He turns around, takes my hand and leads me to the couch. We sit.

"Grace, this is never going to get any easier. We're going to the recital."

"Look, Seamus, Larry will understand, really. It's not that important, and as you can see I'm a bit busy—"

"I need you to help me here, Grace. I need you to get me a pen and paper." I fold my hands in my lap.

"Please, Grace. The notepad you write this stuff in"—his arm makes a sweep of the room—"will be perfect."

My notepad and pen are on the counter. I get them. I flip to a new page and hand them to him. I stand in front of him.

"I'm early, so we'll make it. Now, 2 minutes for your teeth. Say 5 for your shower and 10 for your hair." He's jotting while he speaks. "Get me a clock."

I hand him the digital clock from the top of the bookcase. I don't have a lot of digital clocks; they're useless for most things because they don't show seconds. I just keep a few around because they're easier to see from a distance. He sets it on the kitchen counter.

"Grace, in 2 minutes it'll be 12:00. We're going to start then. See this list? It says you've got 10 minutes to pack up the kitchen. Then you need to get ready, but you must time yourself according to the numbers I've written down here. No longer, no shorter. Exact."

He hands me the notepad. In his neat hand, he has made 4 columns. The first: tasks, like pack up the kitchen and dress. The second: minutes. The third: time at the commencement of the task. The fourth: time at the completion of the task.

My hand swings down to my side, but I don't let go of the pad. "I can't. I don't think I can—"

"The clock's about to tick over, Grace. You need to start at the stroke of 12."

The pain in my chest is gone. I look at the kitchen and for a second I can't remember how it got to be in that state. I stare at the clock, and as I stare I can almost see each little light move from 11:59 to 12:00, as if in

slow motion. And before I know it, I'm moving toward the kitchen.

Seamus drives with one hand on the wheel and his arm out straight. I fall in love with his mastery on the way to the recital. He always checks his mirrors like you're supposed to. I've never considered driving to be sexy, but I must be alone in this because people even consider those effeminate Formula One midgets appealing. The other cars on the road are doing their thing: stopping at red lights, keeping to the speed limit, signaling when they're going to pass. There's a complex set of rules that keeps everything running smoothly. Someone made those rules up, every one of them, and in the end everyone gets to where they want to go.

"Grace," he says, "I want you to tell me . . . about your counting thing. When you had treatment before, they must have had a theory. What causes it?"

"Some people think it's biological. An imbalance in brain chemicals, in the same way that diabetics can't make insulin. No one seems to know the exact reason— perhaps it's genetic." I look out the side window. "The other theory is that it's behavioral or environmental or caused by a trauma. I vote for the brain chemicals with a genetic cause, in which case I can blame my mother."

"And how do they treat it?"

"Behavioral approaches, like relaxation exercises and being forced to not count. They seem to have a reasonable success rate. Also antianxiety drugs and antidepressants."

He parallel parks in front of the school with insolent confidence. I would have hit a tree. He switches the engine off and turns to face me.

"My brother Declan's wife, Megan . . . she's a doctor. I've asked her about it. About you. That's what she told me. She also told me she knows a fantastic psychiatrist and a clinic that does wonderful work. You could go to your GP on Monday and get a referral."

I open my mouth but he speaks again.

"Don't say anything now. Maybe I shouldn't have brought it up but I want you to know you have options and that I'll support you every step. Promise me you'll think about it."

I can see the fair spread across the oval: lots of kids running around, stalls everywhere. A jumping castle. Normal families, normal Saturday. White folding seats set out in front of a stage for the recital. I am here today. I made it out. I will hear my niece play the violin, because of Seamus.

"I'll think about it."

We walk through the school grounds, past children with cotton candy on sticks chasing each other. Children in their best clothes: designer jeans and pastel dresses.

I feel a little self-conscious: I'm dressed in a white skirt and a white top. Not the outfit due today, but Seamus picked it while I was in the shower. It's okay, except the bra (also chosen by Seamus) is black and visible under the white shirt. The white shirt, too, makes my breasts look bigger. This is how women would dress all the time if men chose their clothes, like pneumatically enhanced tea ladies. My hair looks ratty because the 10 minutes he allowed for hair wasn't enough.

At the side of the stage is a group of giggling girls holding musical instruments. At the edge of this group, not giggling, is Larry. I send her a royal wave and walk slower so I can point to Seamus without his seeing. Larry slaps her palm to her forehead.

We sit and almost straightaway 35 children in uniform file across the stage with their instruments. Nikola didn't have children. His friends wanted him to, knowing the world would be a smarter place if he passed his genes on. If he were alive today Nikola could sell his sperm on the Internet, thereby improving mankind without the awkward realities of actual babies. Back at the turn of the century there was no stigma about trying to improve humanity.

Nikola knew that the demands of his work were too encompassing to allow for a wife and children. But a demanding job isn't the only reason to be childless. There's overpopulation. Global warming. Think of the

environmental impact of disposable diapers—8,000 diapers per baby and 500 years for each one to decompose; in Australia, a baby is born every 2 minutes, so 262,800 per year. Times 8,000 nappies is 2.1×10^9. And that's not the worst bit. Feeding it. Clothing it. Being responsible for another person's life. For their whole existence. Get your head around that. There are a million great reasons not to have children.

But sitting here at the recital, holding hands with Seamus and watching Larry play the violin, it's easy to forget them all. She's at the back of the stage, and now that she is lined up with her orchestra mates, it's apparent she doesn't look like the rest of the girls. Her hair is messy and still its natural color, a sandy straw. She doesn't wear any eye makeup or lip gloss. She's not grinning at parents in the front row. Her tongue is between her teeth. Every stroke of her bow is deliberate, precise. She's wonderful.

The recital finishes and miniature black belts flood the stage for a kung fu demonstration. We stand and move to the side of the stage. After a few moments she sees us and rushes over, violin case in one hand. Now they are standing next to each other. Seamus and Larry. She is about 7 centimeters shorter than me, but he towers over us both.

"Larry, this is my friend Seamus. Seamus, the famous Larry."

"Larry, what a pleasure to hear you play. You were clearly the best violin. Rather embarrassing for all the other parents."

She laughs, head down and looking sideways, but doesn't speak.

"Now for lunch. Your choice is hot of dog, in a hand-sliced roll, or burger of ham with tomato sauce garnish," Seamus says, in a horrible French accent. Larry laughs. Seamus offers me his arm. I take Larry's hand.

As we walk, the 3 of us, I think about all the times I've been sick and no one has believed me. Like the time that I caught a train (never doing that again) and someone in the carriage was sneezing and I thought I had meningitis because I had a terrible headache and could've sworn I had purple spots and the nurse at the emergency room barely looked at me. It can be very hard to convince someone you're sick.

It can be equally as hard to convince someone you're well. But, as we wander off to blow the 50 bucks Jill gave me on 3 packets of chocolate fudge, 3 hotdogs with mustard and 15 tickets (C17 pink to C31 pink—everyone knows consecutive tickets are luckier) in a raffle for a lurid patchwork quilt that seems the conception of someone born color-blind and the execution of someone with 3 fingers, I wonder what a baby with Seamus's eyes would look like.

Chapter 12

I am quiet during the drive home. The strange place, strange food and seeing Larry and Seamus together have left me heady and exhausted. Perhaps I'm coming down with something. Seamus is quiet too, until he parks in front of my flat.

"Did you have a good time?" he says.

I lean back in the seat. "Amazing. The best thing I've done in ages."

"There's a whole world out there, you know, Grace. A school recital really shouldn't be the best thing you've done in ages."

"It's complicated."

"It's really not. Prisoners in minimum security have more freedom than you. You deserve more from life than this."

I open the car door, and lean across and kiss his cheek. "Thanks for the ride." I'd like to stay in the car and talk, but I need to go. I have to start preparing dinner in 16 minutes.

After dinner I sit on the edge of my bed and pick up Nikola's photo—he's right-side-up at the moment, but he's spent a lot of time facedown over the last 6 weeks and 1 day since I first met Seamus at the supermarket.

Nikola was sick several times. When he was 25 he became so hypersensitive that he could do nothing but take to his bed. The sound of a bee buzzing in the garden outside his room would explode inside his head—an enormous, cavernous sound. If someone walked in the house the vibrations would magnify up his body until he could hardly bear the shaking. A train traveling through the countryside miles away would rattle his teeth and the root of each hair in his head. His parents installed rubber matting under the legs of his bed so he could sleep. I feel like this sometimes, like each time a number hits me my head recoils and if I were to squeeze one more number into my body they would seep out from my eyeballs and my nose and drizzle from my ears.

This wasn't Nikola's only strange symptom. Since childhood, whenever he became excited he would

see bursts of light before his eyes that momentarily blinded him. Sometimes he actually believed the room in which he stood was on fire. Nikola also had visions, images of things he had seen that were unwilling to lie quietly in his memory. These flashes were often cued by conversations, so if, while chatting to him, you mentioned the word "hammer," he would be confronted by the image of a hammer so vivid it blocked the rest of his sight and took him some time to decide if it was real. If he stretched his hand out in front, the image would close in around it and remain in place. He knew it was unusual. He was worried. He saw doctor after doctor, but none had any idea what made his mind so special.

It may have upset him at the time, but in typical Nikola style he made the most of it. Every invention he made throughout his life, he visualized first. He rarely made models because the images in his head were complete in every way. He could mentally switch on engines and generators and watch them run. He could manipulate them, turn them over and test them. This was one of the reasons he had no partners or colleagues—other engineers wanted blueprints and scale drawings. Nikola had no need.

The images themselves gave him the idea for another invention, one he never made. He believed that

his visions were some kind of projection from the brain onto the retina, and, logically extending this, it should be possible to devise a machine to capture and project them on a screen. In the late 1800s, before the rise of the motion picture and decades before television, Nikola envisaged sharing the scenes from your life with another, like a holiday slide night without the camera.

Just as well Nikola isn't alive now. Imagine a child these days telling a doctor they saw pictures in front of their eyes, pictures so vivid they couldn't differentiate them from reality. Not to mention the counting. It's easy to see what would happen to that poor little boy. Psychiatrists. Behavioral therapists. Drugs. They'd probably say he was schizophrenic or psychotic or something. They would treat him, and all the strange workings of his brain would stop. He would no longer count or have visions. He would never grow up to become an inventor. All that matters to doctors now is that we humans become closer to being the same. Closer to average.

I know about this pressure to conform and have managed to withstand it. When I was in the hospital 25 months ago I was prescribed all kinds of medication. I told the doctors I took it, but I rarely did. Rarely enough for it to have no effect on my personality. Some

of the nurses were conscientious and would watch me swallow, but I learned quickly how to tuck the tablets under my tongue. Others couldn't be bothered checking. They had so much to think about—how many packets of hospital gloves they could slide into their handbag before anyone noticed, the whereabouts of their teenage daughters, the oozing of last night's semen onto their already-stained underwear. It was easy to tip the pills down the sink in my privately insured room.

They told me back then that taking the pills could stop me from counting. Perhaps it could have. But I didn't take the pills because you can never tell—that's the lesson. You never know what is meant to be, what is right, what will eventually save you. I remember sitting in my hospital bed thinking: What would the world have lost if some hospital had "cured" Nikola? If I change myself, how will I be diminished?

But right now, sitting on my bed, I'm not thinking about what the world might have lost. I'm thinking about sitting in a car for as long as I like, going out to dinner, sleeping in on Sundays. I'm thinking about how much I have to gain.

It all happens very fast. In a little over 2 weeks I have appointments with a psychiatrist and a behavioral ther-

apist. I meet the psychiatrist first. Professor Segrove's office is the size of my whole flat but furnished only with a serious bookcase, an enormous oak desk with a green top, two bucket chesterfields and a chesterfield couch. There's no way I'm lying on the couch. Seamus offered to come up with me, but there's not a chance I'll let him. Instead he waits in the car.

Professor Segrove is shiny bald with ferocious eyebrows and wears a red polka-dot bow tie and red suspenders over a white shirt. His gray trousers must be tailored because they are a snug fit around his spherical tummy yet taper down to his skinny ankles and rest atop his tiny handmade shoes. "So, Grace. What brings you here?" He grins mercilessly and pulls on his bow tie. This is a disconcerting habit in a psychiatrist, especially since I've always considered bow ties to be a sign of mental illness, a kind of subliminal desire to garrote oneself.

"Just wondered if you validate parking." 75 books on the top shelf.

He smiles. He nods. "Very good, very good. The referral from the GP says you think it's time to address your counting." He gestures to a folder on his desk. An extraordinary number of stiff white hairs stick straight up out of his eyebrows—possibly redirected hairs that have abandoned his head. They move so erratically

when he speaks that I lose count and have to start again. Almost impossible to be sure, but I think 15 left, 17 right.

"That's a big step," he continues. "How old were you when you started to count?"

I nearly say I was 3 years old, like everyone, but I've come all this way. Seamus has taken a half day off work to drive me. I cross my legs. Then I uncross them and cross them the other way.

"To varying degrees, since I was 8."

Professor Segrove leans forward and grins, hands on his chin. He is enthusiastic, like a pimply boy at McDonald's who beams because, yes, you would like fries with that. It's frightening to see someone who so loves his work.

He looks at the folder again. "I see here you've been hospitalized once before. Was this when the counting began to interfere with your life?"

"Yes. 25 months ago." Only 45 books on the second shelf. Fatter ones.

"25 months ago." He's taking notes now, writing on a fat wad of plain paper, and still grinning. Why on earth is he grinning like that? This can't be that much fun. Does he imagine I will become fodder for an academic paper in *New Shrink Monthly*? "The baffling case of Grace V"?

"Grace, you've done very well. Often the most difficult part for people with obsessive-compulsive disorder is actually beginning treatment, because it's such a change to their normal routine. Often people cancel their first appointments."

Often people are smarter than I am.

"It was a difficult night last night. I . . ." I dig my fingers into the leather of the chair. "I measured all the dimensions . . . the walls . . . of my apartment. Then I wrote the numbers on the walls. Seamus, my boyfriend . . . he came over to help at 2:00 A.M. Actually 2:09 A.M." I don't mention how soothing it was to see those numbers on the walls this morning. Whatever happens, I'm keeping them.

He writes this down. The poor thing is probably stuck in a loveless marriage, living in a cold, empty house in Kew or Canterbury paying private school fees for a child he doesn't realize isn't his. If a woman who writes numbers on her walls is so exciting—well, this can be my good deed for the week. He stands up, walks to the bookcase (can't count the bottom shelf from here), then sits down again.

I try not to think about how many other perfectly well people have sat in this handsome chesterfield with 19 dimples on the backrest. About how many other innocent little quirks Professor Segrove—no first name

on the door, not even an initial, though he looks like a Julius—is working so hard to expel. Fussy eater? Can't stand chicken? "Come, my chicken-loathing friend. I will cure you!" Cry at old movies or phone company ads where the handsome Italian son calls Mamma back in the village? Arise, and walk! Soon you shall cast aside your obvious depressive illness with possible borderline personality tendencies and become as hard-hearted as the rest of us, able to watch the 6 o'clock news every day without so much as a twinge of compassion! In the hands of Professor Segrove we will all become normal.

"How do you feel if you can't count things?"

Like I've got every disease known to man and a few that haven't been discovered yet. "Anxious, I suppose. Sometimes."

As if no one else in the world ever worries. Nikola had enormous challenges, things that seemed impossible at the time, dreams even bigger than electricity. Today, with TV, radio, mobile phone and Bluetooth signals zipping around us continually, it's easy to underestimate the genius behind the vision. But imagine the world in 1900, with none of those things. Queen Victoria is still on the throne. Australia isn't even a country. Women don't have the vote.

Professor Segrove grins again, takes a clean piece of paper and draws a smiley face. He holds it up, facing

me. If Mr. Smiley had eyebrows it would look exactly like him. "Together we will build a staircase to a healthier future, Grace." He scribbles again and hands me a prescription.

My first meeting with the behavioral therapist is straight after my appointment with Professor Segrove. In the waiting room are 15 chairs. I sit and wait. I hope Seamus has found a coffee shop somewhere. "It's no trouble," he said, when I told him about the appointments. "I'd be delighted to take you."

What Nikola imagined was a radio communications tower capable of reaching most of the United States and across the Atlantic. He imagined news bulletins, stock market updates, telephone networks—everything we have today. He was more than 100 years ahead of his time. One small problem: to build his tower he needed money. Westinghouse couldn't help, so Nikola turned to the one man who had the cash. The billionaire industrialist J. Pierpont Morgan.

When Morgan heard what Nikola had to offer, even he was astounded. Imagine, Mr. Capitalist, a worldwide monopoly on radio stations. I have already successfully transmitted over 700 miles, Nikola told him. It will only cost you $350,000 all up: $100,000 for the first transmitter to cover the Atlantic and another $250,000 to

cover the Pacific. Morgan advanced Nikola $150,000; plenty to get started. Nikola was thrilled and promised a hundredfold return on the investment. To start to build his dream, Nikola now needed land.

"Grace Vandenburg? Yes?" A woman appears from behind the counter. She is tall and thin with black hair so lank it looks damp, reminiscent of an oil spill slicked down her cheeks. Her clothes are 1920s retro: a gray dropped-waist shift over a white shirt, shiny black shoes with a buckle at the ankle.

No. Nope. Never heard of her. I'm just here to service the photocopier.

"I'm Francine. Please follow me."

Francine leads me, shiny black shoes clopping with every step, to a meeting room that is empty except for a circle of plastic chairs. I cross my arms and my legs. Then I think perhaps this looks like a defensive posture, so I uncross them. I look for a window to jump out of but there's none.

"Welcome, welcome. I'll be leading both your group sessions and your individual therapy sessions. I know it's a little awkward now but believe me, we'll be the best of friends in no time." Her forehead is permanently creased in a frown of caring and concern.

Actually my friends register is full. I could fit you in but someone else would have to die first.

"Now, first I want to ask about your personal support network."

Huh?

"Your friends, family. People who understand you are beginning to climb the staircase to a healthier future, and will give you a hand up, so to speak."

That bloody staircase again. "Well, there's my boyfriend. He's very supportive. He drove me today."

Francine's forehead becomes a furrow so deep I fear it will dent her brain. Or perhaps it already has. "No one else? Girlfriends? Family?"

Sorry. Raised by wolves.

"There's my mother and sister. I haven't told them about . . . the staircase."

"Tsk-tsk-tsk."

I have never met anyone who actually makes a "tsk" sound. I wonder if it takes much practice. My tongue involuntarily prods my hard palate but I'll have to wait until I get home to try.

"Our family and friends are our handrails, as it were. It's vital you tell them. Vital. I know Professor Segrove agrees."

This is my golden opportunity to ask Professor Segrove's first name, but I suddenly think: What if "Professor" is his first name, like Major Major in *Catch-22*? His parents might have been farsighted,

planning for young Professor's future career advancement. Francine takes advantage of my pause to deliver further instructions.

"This is what you do, Grace. In your journal—you do have a journal, don't you?"

I snort. "Of course. I have 100 back copies of the *Journal of the American Medical Association*."

Francine's eyes bulge. "No, no, Grace. A journal. Like a diary. You must have a journal. This is vital. Use your journal to describe your day-to-day struggles, so that when you are halfway up your staircase you can look back and see how far you've come. Your sense of personal achievement will help you through your darkest days. Also, make a list of people you need to tell about your treatment. You can make a heading: 'Sharing List.'"

"'Sharing List'? Are you certain? Can't I call it 'Support List' instead?"

Francine tilts her head to the side. "Well . . . it's a little unorthodox, but . . . tell you what, Grace. You go ahead and call it 'Support List' and I'll check with Professor Segrove. If there's any problem, I'll ring you. But the heading must be on page one. Family support is vital, Grace. Repeat to yourself: honesty and acceptance will help build my staircase."

When I get back to the car, Seamus is waiting with a take-out coffee and the paper. He likes to read every

word of the sports pages. He doesn't see me as I approach. On the right side of his head is a patch of hair that grows to the side, rather than straight down. I know what this patch feels like. I've felt it with my fingers.

"Hey," I say.

He starts and gets out of the car. "Hey yourself. How did it go?"

"I'm cured."

He walks around the front of the car to open my door. "Seriously. How did it go?"

"Get ready for the highlight of your existence," I say. "You're at the top of my support list." When he opens the door, I kiss him.

So tonight, Wednesday, I start at the top of my list and ring my mother.

"Goodness, Grace. I haven't missed a Sunday, have I? Are you well?"

"No, Mum. It's not Sunday yet. And yes, I'm fine. I'm just . . ."

"Yes?"

Take a breath. "I've decided . . . to try therapy. I'm seeing . . . a psychiatrist . . . about . . . the counting thing."

"Really, dear? Again? After all this time? I thought you said you were happy. You were always insistent that you were happy."

"I am." Take another breath. "But I guess I could be happier."

"I suppose it can't hurt, but I want you to be careful. Psychiatrists aren't right in the head, you know, dear. You know what Tom Cruise says. I remember reading that psychiatrists have the highest suicide rate of any profession. Or was it dentists? If it was dentists I could understand. Who would want to spend all day with their hands in other people's mouths? Quite revolting. Even worse in the old days before gloves. I remember a dentist I once had who was a smoker. I could smell it on his hands. Disgusting. A friend of mine had all her mercury fillings extracted and she's as right as rain now. Are your bowels regular?"

She is sweet, loving and accepting. I am conscious of millions of my brain cells atrophying as she speaks. I am certainly not talking to my mother about my bowels, in case she reciprocates.

Next, I ring Jill.

"Grace? It's a Wednesday. Is everything all right?"

"Jill . . . I've decided . . . to try therapy. I'm seeing . . . a psychiatrist . . . about the counting thing . . . Hello? Jill? Are you still there?"

"Yes . . . I'm here. Are you sure you want to do this? Remember what you said after the last time? 'Why should I see a doctor?' you said. 'I'm not sick. My mind

is an expression of the variety of the human experience,' you said. In fact, I seem to recall you bit my head off when I suggested you try a different psychologist."

"I remember. I remember what I said."

"You said therapy is an attempt to force round pegs into square holes. That individuality is a blessing, not a curse."

"I know, I know."

" 'Medicalization of diversity benefits no one but multinational drug companies with a vested interest in enlarging the definition of illness,' you said." This from a woman who takes 30 minutes to find her 4-wheel drive in the Southland parking lot. All of a sudden she's digitally recorded every single statement I've uttered in the past year.

"Jill, I know. I know what I said. But the past is the past. I'm trying therapy now."

"Well, if you're sure. If it makes you happy. Remember what we told you last time; Harry and I are happy to help. Financially I mean."

Wow. And I'm not even a tax-deductible charity. Just saying it must give her a warm glow. "Thanks anyway."

"It's your new boyfriend, isn't it? Seamus. When do we get to meet him? Hilly says he's very nice. He must be worth it."

—————

On my way home from the café next morning I make two detours: the newsstand, to buy my journal, and the pharmacy to fill the prescription. I choose a plain exercise book—white pages, blue lines. The ones with kittens on the cover are not for me. In the pharmacy I try not to calculate how much money the drug company is making from me.

I try, too, not to wonder if this drug is the same one they prescribe to people who shop too much. The same one they make flavored and colored for depressed children. As the efficient woman in white makes a label with my name on it and sticks it on the box (that must be a rewarding career after 6 years at university) I'm tempted to ask her if she can also sell me the drug to make me thin. She'd know the one—the one that prevents you from absorbing the fat you eat, so instead it leaks out of your anus later. I am also tempted to ask about a drug to make me tanned, and another to cut down the amount of sleep I need. And then, when I'm a skinny superwoman who sleeps for 4 hours a night she might recommend a plastic surgeon so I can pay more money to look as average as I feel.

The following Monday it's 24 degrees. I start the group therapy sessions in the same room where I first

met Francine. When I arrive at precisely 4:00 P.M. she's waiting, this time in a mole-colored boatneck smock. Same shoes—from this angle I can see them better. Tap shoes. That explains the clipping and clopping last week. We sit opposite each other in our awkward plastic circle. There are 5 empty chairs.

"It's good to see you, Grace. Most people find the group sessions a rewarding and enlightening part of the process."

"I bet they do."

"Do you have your journal yet?"

I'm tempted to tell her the dog ate my homework, but instead I pull my exercise book from its plastic bag and wave it.

Francine briefly examines it, then nods. "Grace . . . we have had a little bit of trouble finding people with . . . similar challenges to yours. You might not be aware but yours is quite an unusual variation."

" 'Unusual' is my middle name."

"So, rather than delay your therapy, we've decided to include you in our standard obsessives group. Ah, here they are now. Edith, Daria. Gemma. Carla. Gary. This is Grace. We're all here. Welcome. Please take a seat."

Easier said than done. Edith, early twenties with corkscrew blonde ringlets, white tank top and skinny

jeans, wears gloves and chooses the seat next to mine, but doesn't sit yet. She removes a parcel from her green shopping bag: a floral pillowcase covered in plastic wrap. Using only one hand, she unwraps it and lays it on the seat, lining up the edges with NASA precision. She carefully returns the plastic wrap to her bag, and then unpacks another pair of gloves: black cotton like the ones on her hands. She removes her old gloves and pulls on the new ones in movements choreographed so her skin touches nothing but glove. She sits.

Daria and Gemma both have perfect olive skin and shiny dark hair; they could be sisters. Daria is perhaps in her early forties, Gemma could almost be fifty. They even dress similarly: tailored pants, one navy and one chocolate, and flowing peasant-style tops, one white and one floral, with sleeves that reach beyond their fingertips. They choose seats opposite each other in our little circle, then each pulls from her bag a fresh folded newspaper, spreads the inside pages on her seat and sits on them.

Gemma gives a tight smile. "Unopened newsprint truly is 'hot off the presses,' you know. It's most unlikely to be contaminated."

Carla, a matronly woman in a pink knitted suit, has small rectangular glasses and bouffant blonde hair. Her hands are a collage of pink, glistening fresh. She nods

to each of us and produces a bottle of disinfectant and a wad of cotton balls. She begins swabbing her chair.

This leaves Gary. Dark, tall, thinning hair. Glasses too round for his pudgy face. Jeans, a crumpled T-shirt and sneakers. Late thirties, but out of shape. Perhaps he is absentminded since he's brought no supplies. He sits on his hands.

Great. Hand washers. Me and a room full of nut-bags.

"Welcome, everyone. This session is really a 'get to know you.' A time to feel comfortable with each other. Share the difficulties we face and swap little tips and hints."

Carla, who has finished dousing her chair, sits and immediately raises her hand.

"Yes, Carla?"

Carla turns to Gary. "Touching the chair with the skin of your hands is very dangerous. The germs climb onto your hands and run right up your arms until they reach your head."

Gary leaps up like his chair has spontaneously com-busted, shaking his hands at the blue-tinged wrists. He nods several times at Carla, but whether out of re-spect for a superior nutbag or resentment I can't tell. He hangs his head and stands behind his chair. The others squirm in their seats. Different ages, sexes,

habits, and the same psychosis. They seem to have a natural affinity, like the members of a rock band. The Germphobics, perhaps.

Daria raises her hand. Francine beams acknowledgment.

"Daria. Thank you for breaking the ice."

"I found a terrific shop in Preston that sells those little steel tongs with rubber tips. You know the ones . . . you can seal them in a Ziploc bag straight from the dishwasher and carry them around all day. I use them to eat potato chips and open doors and shake hands. I always carry at least three." She pulls a sample pair, asphyxiated in the closed position, from her bag.

"Thank you for sharing, Daria," says Francine. "I respect the courage it takes to be the first to speak. But what we're really looking for are tips and hints to help us fight our obsessions. But thank you for sharing anyway."

Gemma raises her hand. "I've recently learned you can thread an apple with string using a large darning needle so you can hold it under boiling water and then suspend it from a doorway until you're ready to eat it, all without using your hands."

Almost before Gemma finishes, Daria's hand is up again. She waves her flowing white top. "I use the

fabric of my sleeve to open doors. I can also turn on taps using my elbow.

"Again, thank you, Gemma and Daria, for those helpful tips. I know a good one: everyone could try wearing a tight rubber band around their wrist. Each time you think an obsessive thought, give your rubber band a flick. Negative reinforcement."

Daria screws up her face at Gemma. "I can flush a toilet using my foot." Even Francine stares.

"It's not so hard," Daria says. "I've been practicing."

By the time I get home I'm exhausted. Seamus makes me spaghetti with too much chili and tells me how wonderful I am, how brave. I manage to eat 30 strands. After dinner, we make love and like most things the more we practice the better we become. My body feels like a vessel in his hands and by itself my skin responds. When he suckles my nipples my breasts grow fuller and heavier with a sweet ache that makes me gasp. When we make love my uterus moves lower, suddenly and irrevocably aware of its hollowness.

Afterward his head nestles in the concave part of my shoulder, a space made just for this.

"Tell me a story," I say.

"About what?"

"Did you always want to work in a cinema?"

He laughs. "It wasn't my childhood dream. But when I was a teenager I was always more interested in football and surfing and hanging around with my mates. Still am. I love movies. The job is okay. The people I work with are great. Then I go home."

"Growing up with a sister and 3 brothers. What was it like?"

"Noisy. Crazy. 4 wild boys and a sick little girl, 2 impossibly busy parents."

"Sounds like fun."

"It was out of control. I'll give you an example: we used to play a game called snap for slaps. It was the same as the regular card game but the winner was entitled to slap his loser brother as hard as he could."

"Wow. Mob rule."

"Absolutely. The number one law in the household was to never leave your plate unattended. If your brother ate your dinner you'd be hungry until morning."

"So did you suffer many slaps and hungry nights?"

He laughs again and I can feel it inside the cavity of my chest. "Until a stroke of good luck. My greatest love as a kid was Superman comics. One day I jumped from the shed roof with a bedsheet as a cape."

My fingers tighten in his hair. "Were you hurt?"

"Mild concussion, broken arm. But it was a life-changing event. The cast was like armor. Suddenly I was king of the street. Some of the kids used to pick on Kyles. Not after I broke my arm they didn't."

It's as if little Seamus is right there in front of me, standing to the left of the bed. I can see him now. He is 4 years old. He has brown hair and devoted eyes. I can see the cast on his right arm and the shadow of a black eye from fighting. This boy risks everything to defend his sister. He was a rescuer before he met me.

Seamus falls asleep resting on my shoulder. My arm is around him, and I hold him a little tighter after hearing about his fall. When he was a small child, Nikola's brother Dane was killed in an accident. A fall from a horse. Nikola always blamed himself and perhaps it was his fault. Perhaps he upset the horse, making him shy and rear. Nikola never recovered from his brother's death. He always said Dane was the talented one, the exceptional one, and that he spent his whole life working to ease his parents' loss.

Nikola's new project was to become the pinnacle of his life. He bought farmland on Long Island and named it Wardenclyffe. He commissioned an architect to design an enormous octagonal wood and brick tower almost 200 feet tall, with a roof like a giant copper cap 100 feet across. The projected cost was astronomical,

but Nikola wasn't fazed. He had Morgan's money, and his patronage. Nothing could go wrong.

When my lids grow heavy I roll Seamus onto his side and snuggle up behind him. As I fall asleep I dream of all the empty parts of my body. I dream of the chambers of my heart between pulses and my bladder and my throat and the hollows of my ears and my nose. The tiny empty bubbles of my lungs. I dream that these join together with my empty uterus and fill all of me, so that 4 millimeters under my skin I am entirely hollow. In my dream I have always been hollow but I didn't realize it until now.

Nothing can go wrong with my therapy. The professor and Francine are trying so hard it would be churlish of me not to change.

After a few days on the medication I develop the weirdest sensation of having two brains—one in charge of abstract thoughts and concepts and the other in charge of my body. If I want to walk or scratch my nose, my two brains have to sit down together in the crimson-upholstered room that is my actual brain and discuss it. They sit facing each other across a large walnut desk. The abstract brain, who is very polite, asks the practical brain if she would very much mind moving my leg. And the physical brain, similarly charming and eager to please, is delighted to assist.

Luckily they are fast talkers, so my leg can do its thing in a fraction of a second. No one even knows about the delay except us three.

And the medication is working. I don't feel like counting. I can barely find any numbers in the crimson-upholstered room, either on the desk or around the chairs. Unless there are cupboards in there, hidden behind the upholstery. If my two brains know where the numbers are, they aren't telling.

Chapter 13

Francine does cognitive behavioral therapy too. The day of my first session I have a splitting headache like my two brains have decided they never really liked each other after all and have dropped any semblance of politeness and instead begun attacking each other and the crimson-upholstered room with chain saws. I think the fight is about who is more abstract and who is more practical. What a pair of juvenile half-brains.

Francine speaks like a children's television host, her soggy hair ebbing as her head flops with sympathy. I half expect a glove puppet to pop up beside her, calling her Miss Francine and suggesting she read us a story. I had been forewarned about cognitive behavioral therapy. A few days before Gemma had pulled me aside

and told me about her first individual session in hushed tones, how she was shepherded to the clinic toilet and forced to watch Francine dip an apple in the toilet bowl and then eat it.

The Germphobics have two theories about Francine. The first is that anyone who eats dinner at her house is making a grave error. The second is that, because Francine has obviously done this before with similar groups of right-thinking, clean-living people, she has built up immunity to toilet-bowl germs over time. Francine indulged in apple *à la toilette* for nothing; the Germphobics remain convinced that this little experiment would kill a normal person.

My behavioral therapy is more challenging. In my personal equivalent of apple dunking, Francine puts me in circumstances where it's almost impossible not to count. She deals playing cards in front of me, faceup. She arranges coins and buttons and matchsticks in piles and pyramids. She asks me to bring in my Cuisenaire rods and she spreads them in front of me and together we make little patterns. She is vigilant in checking for any tapping of the foot or clicking of the tongue or moving of the lip, but truthfully I'm not in the mood.

Francine says that, when I'm ready, I should throw the rods away. They devised this, Francine and Professor Professor together, as a symbol of my new

202 · TONI JORDAN

non-counting state because it's so much harder to control my thoughts than the Germphobics' behaviors.

So just like that, one Wednesday a few weeks after my sessions began, I stand up from behind Francine's desk. I walk to the wastepaper bin in the corner. I drop them in. I could have done something more flamboyant. I'm sure, the way I used to think, I could have organized a ceremonial burning or discarded one rod a day to signify my healthy staircase. But in the end it seems childish to have held on to that tired plastic box with its wooden sticks. They were so old, the box even had a crack down one side. The rods were faded and the paint was thinning on the edges. After I trash them I go home and watch TV.

Eventually it will all have to go, they say: the numbers written on my cupboards and drawers, my notebook, the clocks. Removing these things will prove that I finally understand the harm numbers did me. That they are the source of my distress. Then Francine will help me get a part-time job.

Seamus stays over often, and I love it. He's earning that spot on the top of my support list. He even reminds me to take my medication. One weekend Seamus and I wear our oldest clothes (although I can't tell the difference because he still wears faded jeans and a polo shirt), move all the furniture, cover everything with drop cloths and paint out the num-

bers on the walls. We paint everything plain white. He chose it. I couldn't be bothered picking a color. I don't count the brushstrokes. As we paint the brains chat with Seamus.

Seamus: Where are your rods?

Brain One: My what?

Seamus: Your Cuisenaire rods. They're usually right here on the bedside table.

Brain Two: What did happen to those?

Brain One: I threw them out.

Seamus: Really? You threw them out? You've had them since you were, what, eight?

Brain Two: Ish.

Brain One: Or thereabouts.

Seamus: Why on earth did you throw them out?

Brain Two: Yes, why?

Brain One: Francine told me to. Plus, I was over them.

Seamus: God, they made you do that? That's a bit rough.

Brain Two: You're telling me. We're going to regret losing them for the rest of our life.

Brain One: Speak for yourself. Onward and upward, I say. Take no prisoners.

Seamus: You've been working so hard on this, Grace. I know it's not easy, these early stages. I

know you're tired and you have trouble concen-
trating, but you need to be patient. We both do.
Tell you what, when you finish the therapy, let's
take a holiday.

Brain Two: A holiday? That would be terrific.

Brain One: Terrific, terrific. Where would we go?

Seamus: Anywhere you want. Just lie on a beach if
you want. Or somewhere more exciting.

Brain One: Lie on a beach! Lie on a beach!

Brain Two: Somewhere more exciting! Somewhere
more exciting!

Brain One: We'll give it some thought.

Seamus: We?

Brain One: You. And me.

This is exactly the life I want. I want to take holi-
days and be with Seamus and live a normal life. I don't
mind the loss of these pointless things: ink on paper
and walls, bits of wood. I am enormously improved
and delighted with my two brains. It is infinitely
more sensible having two. Perhaps, a few short weeks
ago at the beginning of my therapy, I was possibly a
bit harsh toward the professor and Francine and the
Germphobics. Possibly I've been a tad unkind toward
people in general, but now my brains and I are suffused
with a gentler, live-and-let-live philosophy. I begin to

have longer conversations with my mother, and she totally fails to irritate me.

One Sunday night she rings me as usual. I'm not exactly sure what time it is.

Mother: So how are you, dear?

Brain One: You answer.

Brain Two: No, you answer.

Brain One: Fine. Thanks.

Mother: Jill says you have a boyfriend.

Brain One: Yes. He's Irish.

Mother: That's wonderful, dear. He's not in that IRA, is he? I've seen them on *60 Minutes*. They seem nice boys but they're not. Is he a comedian?

Brain One: Is who a comedian? Who is she talking about?

Brain Two: She's talking about Seamus.

Brain One: Oh! No, he's not a comedian. He's not in the IRA either.

Mother: Because it seems that every second comedian on television these days is Irish. How do they all get visas, do you think? Imagine how much funnier they would be if you could work out what they were actually saying. They're absolutely incoherent, but very funny. Very

funny people, the Irish. Except the IRA of course. They're not funny at all. Why are there no Russian comedians, do you think?

Now that my mother is making sense it's much easier to have a conversation with her. I wonder if she's on medication. If she is, it's a blessing. Straight after mother hangs up, Jill phones. She's also a lot less irritable. Perhaps she's feeling more relaxed. It must be stressful having children.

Jill: Hello, Gracie. How are you feeling?
Brain One: Good.
Brain Two: Fine.
Jill: I'm calling about the patchwork quilt.
Brain Two: What's a patchwork quilt?
Brain One: I know, I know! Let me handle this.
Jill: Grace? Grace, are you there?
Brain One: Yes. I'm here. I know about the patchwork quilt.
Jill: How could you possibly know? I only found out myself today.
Brain One: You only found out today? They've been making them for years. What happens is, all the leftover little bits of material after you make a dress, instead of throwing them away—

Jill: Grace, please. You are very amusing but I have a million things to do today and . . . I'm calling about the raffle.

Brain Two: I know, I know! Let me answer. You messed up the quilt answer.

Brain One: Unkind and unfair. I told you I'm handling this. Will you please sit us down? Our legs are tired. Now, what raffle?

Jill: The raffle you bought the tickets in when you went to the recital last month.

Brain One: Tickets?

Brain Two: Recital?

Brain One: I don't think I went to a receptacle last month.

Jill: Recital! It was a recital, and Hilary was playing the violin! When Harry and I were in China. And you did go, you and Seamus and . . . Oh, for heaven's sake. You've won first prize: a patchwork quilt. Do you want it or not?

Brain Two: Say yes! Say yes! I want a quill! I want a quill!

Brain One: Yes. Thank you.

Jill: Right. I'll drop it over on my way home from Pilates.

Which astonishes me because I didn't realize she was taking flying lessons. Still, she's so busy and she does

such a wonderful job raising those adorable children, surely she's allowed to do anything she wants in her spare time. She's always been such a wonderful sister to me.

In fact, the next day she drops around for a visit and gives me this fabulous bedspread made up of heaps of beautiful little squares of material sewn together. By hand. And it isn't even my birthday.

The only problem is that, since I've been taking the pills, I'm not entirely sure exactly how long it's been now, Seamus and I haven't been making love. As often. Or at all. It's not that I don't want to, but I haven't been in the mood. He's been wonderful, absolutely wonderful. He holds me and says he understands and it's because my chemistry is having a shake-up. Brain One is incredibly relieved, but Brain Two is a bit shitty. Which is unreasonable because it's all Brain Two's fault. When he touches me it takes a while for Brain Two to tell Brain One that he's touched me. For instance, when Seamus puts his hand on my left breast, Brain Two feels it. Brain Two then says to Brain One: He's put his hand on our left breast. Brain One says: Really? Are you sure? Brain Two says: Almost positive. Brain One then says: Great! I really like it when he does that. So there's a delay while they chat about

it. There's a lot of pressure. And there's one other teeny problem. I can't orgasm anymore.

I used to be very good at orgasms. Fast and efficient since my adolescence because at any moment my mother could walk into my room without knocking. But now it's like I'm hiking toward a mountain in the distance and I can see it very clearly, its trees and crevices and snowcapped peak, but no matter how fast I walk, the mountain always seems a little bit farther away and I walk faster but now it's even farther away and I start running but it never comes any closer until I get bored and I stop. And then I have a chocolate cookie. Luckily Seamus doesn't seem to mind. At all. In fact, we hardly ever go to bed at the same time anymore. Most nights he stays up late and watches TV. I don't even hear him come to bed.

This little problem would be the ideal thing to discuss in group session, but I can't bring myself to raise it. It's the Germphobics. I feel so bad for them, the poor things. They don't like sex at all because it's so disgusting, and the more I hear them talk, the more I realize they have a point. I mean, the absurdity of what you need to stick where. And the noises, etc.

When I ask the professor about it, he says all medicines have side effects. Sometimes they are serious. Most of the time they are not. If side effects persist

we can look at varying my medication, or I may need additional treatment. At any time please feel free to ask him or my pharmacist any questions. So that's okay.

And Tesla isn't here anymore. I mean I still have the photo next to my bed because they haven't told me I have to throw it out. But now it's a picture of a dead guy. With a funny mustache. I've never liked men with mustaches. There's something missing that I can't quite put my finger on. Not from the mustache. From my life. Perhaps I should get a flatmate. Normal people have flatmates. Although I'm pretty sure that after all the therapy Seamus and I will move in together and maybe we'll get married. We'll probably have a baby. So a flatmate isn't such a great idea. I might need a dog. Dogs aren't very hygienic, as I've recently learned, liable to carry leptospirosis and rabies, but I believe you can train them to stick their little feet in a disinfectant bath before they come inside. You can also buy shoes for them. Dogs aren't as clean as cats, which need to make sure they don't smell because they hunt individually by stealth, not in a pack like dogs do. It wouldn't do for dinner to smell them coming. Perhaps I need a goldfish.

Outside my kitchen window is a tree I've never noticed before. Its bark is a pale gray, and it's covered in a greenish, crusty growth. Does this mean the tree

is sick? Its leaves are a tired burgundy and they are so sparse. Every breeze seems to bring more down.

Lichen. It's called lichen. Thank God.

I find myself sitting and staring out the window and I'm astonished to realize hours have passed. It's the same when I watch television. Television used to irritate me, the way pleasant shop assistants and helpful waiters did. But now I can stare at it for hours without a thought popping into either of my heads. It's so relaxing, like vodka injected into a vein. I understand why people do it, but I need a bigger set. My tiny portable hardly seems adequate. Now I want a plasma screen the size of a wall.

There are a lot of things I've never noticed before. I nod and smile at my neighbors when we pass in the hall and sometimes we chat about the weather. I've obviously always had neighbors, but I don't recall ever noticing them before. They're nice people: Len and Louise, a lovely couple with matching hairstyles and clothes; Craig and Deborah (he's much taller than she is); and a sweet little old lady called Muriel. A group of Indian students who collectively offered to fix my computer anytime. A career girl called Rose who looks like she stepped out of a fashion magazine.

Which reminds me. I must do something about the way I look. I'd never noticed before but now I seem so old. Fat. My clothes are like rags. Too-tight rags.

Clothes are different now too. Why on earth do girls wear those sunglasses that make them look like flies? I want a pair. It's been years since I bought any clothes, but recently I've somehow gained quite a bit of weight. I don't know how—I still walk most days and unless I'm cooking for Seamus I just have cheese on toast for dinner. I am ravenous, though, all the time. I suppose I do snack a teeny weeny bit. All my clothes are suddenly too tight, so I take the bus to Chadstone and buy some new things. Luckily the lovely shop assistant helps me choose—she is so kind, she pulls out dress after dress and I try them all. I'm not sure my new clothes are right; as soon as I get home I can barely remember buying them. Imagine wide belts being back.

In our group therapy sessions lately we've been discussing going back to work. Francine wants me to tell the story of . . . what happened when I finished work. The Germphobics are fascinated. To them, being a teacher is one of the worst jobs imaginable because kids are little germ factories and being a teacher increases your chances of getting ringworm and nits. I loved being a teacher. I loved those little minds. Even when they were rebelling they were so full of fight.

Francine: Sharing thoughts, feelings and experiences with others helps us all heal. Grace?

How about sharing the story of your break-
down?

Brain One: My breakdown? I don't even drive
anymore.

Brain Two: She means Daniel Deluca.

Brain One: Oh! Daniel Deluca. Sure. No problem.
Easy peasy. I was on playground duty one morn-
ing. On roster. It was hot. There were no clouds.
Kids were running around like crazy. Then I
heard a scream.

Francine: You're doing very well, Grace. Go on.

I go on. It's amazing. I hardly know the Germphobics
or Francine, yet I can sit here in our plastic circle and
tell them this story I've never even told Seamus. But
these days so many of my memories seem like they
happened to someone else or I saw them on television.
So it's easy to recount them, but hard to find the words
to describe exactly what I want to say. I don't want to
sound ridiculous.

Brain One: Anyway it seems so ridiculous now.

Francine: Nothing is ridiculous. We are all here to
help.

Brain One: A little boy from grade two fell off
the jungle gym headfirst and broke his nose.
That's all. His name was Daniel Deluca; that's

a name that's hard to forget. For some reason it was upsetting—there was a lot of blood, but all teachers have seen blood before.

Gemma: Blood? Did any of it touch you?

Brain One: Yes. No. I don't think so. Anyway the little bugger was screaming his lungs out so there can't have been anything seriously wrong with him.

Daria: How much blood? Did it get on your clothes?

Francine: You're doing very well, Grace. Keep going.

Brain One: I tried to keep going, but somehow moving became difficult. Impossible. Sitting down, even moving an arm, was too hard. Limbs like concrete. It was freaky. There was no choice but to stand there. Shock, probably.

Francine: And what happened then?

Brain One: Then one of the kids got another teacher—very stupid because everything would have been fine after a few more minutes.

Time to adjust, that's all that was needed. But when Sharon Liddy the gym teacher arrived, this made things worse because having someone there meant there was no need to recover. Anyway if Sharon had not over-

reacted and had arranged a cup of tea and perhaps a chair everything would have been fine and I wouldn't be here now.

Francine: Did they call an ambulance?

Brain One: They called an ambulance. Two, actually. One for Daniel Deluca. Paramedics should be trained better than to restrain a perfectly well woman. They had the very best of intentions, clearly, but a little time to recover was all that was required. The rest is a bit of a blur.

Gemma: You didn't get in the ambulance? God, they transport people with all kinds of infections in ambulances.

Daria: I'd sooner get in a taxi.

Carla: I have to go and wash my hands.

Francine: "A blur" is not good enough, Grace. You need to try harder.

Brain One: I tried harder when I got to the hospital. I must have seemed better because they let me go home.

Hospitals are more au fait with diagnosing actual problems as opposed to minor shock, so my release was no surprise. Getting home is hazy; perhaps I took a tram. I do remember feeling so tired I couldn't do my

nighttime regime. I changed into my pajamas and went straight to bed.

Francine: Then the next morning things got worse?

Brain One: The next morning things got worse. The alarm was set for 5:55 A.M. as usual, leaving five minutes to wake completely. Getting up time was exactly 6:00 A.M. That used to be quite important.

Brain Two: Can we have a piece of cake?

Brain One: Later.

Brain Two: How much later? I'm starving.

Francine: Continue please, Grace. What happened later?

Brain One: Later . . . I mean earlier . . . during the night there was a power failure—

Gary: What are the chances of that?

Brain Two: I used to know.

Brain One: —a horrible coincidence after the events of the day before. So there was no alarm. Nothing. Only flashing zeros.

Francine: So what did you do?

Brain One: I did nothing. It is impossible to know when to get up when there is nothing to tell you. I lay still.

It wasn't stressful at all. It was peaceful. The numbers had always been there since childhood, but up till then life had worked its way around them. This was when the numbers took over, finally and completely. It was a release.

Francine: And then what happened?

Brain Two: Is it later yet? They sell muffins in the cafeteria.

Brain One: I'm peckish too. At least, by the time Jill came around to check on me, I hadn't eaten for twenty-four hours. It took her a while because the school had to go through their records to find out who to ring when I didn't show for work. It might have been late afternoon, by the light coming in the windows. I'd wet the bed a few times by then—

Gemma: Wet? The bed?

Daria: And you were lying in it?

This wasn't as bad as it seemed. The sticky feeling seemed to bond flesh to sheet to mattress, which was important as getting up was out of the question. Also it was warm. There was no leaving the bed—not for Jill, despite her reasoning and pleading. Poor Jill received no reply at all. There was no getting up for the

ambulance either. All they had to do was set the clock at 5:55 A.M., but of course they couldn't know that. They had to rely on sedation because it's hard to move an unwilling body, even for two big paramedics.

Francine: They took you back to the hospital?

Brain Two: Who died and put you in charge of the muffins anyway?

Brain One: Please be quiet. I'm speaking.

Brain Two: Well, if Carla can wash her hands every two seconds I don't know why I can't nip down to the cafeteria for a muffin.

Francine: And we're listening, Grace. Would you feel better if we held hands?

Gemma: No!

Carla: If anyone touches me they'll be sorry.

Brain Two: Now? How about now?

Brain One: Now, waking up in the hospital moved everything to another level because the rules suddenly became much stricter. I couldn't control my daily routine at all and as the professor explained to me, the numbers had at least been something that I could control.

Somehow the skill of counting quietly was gone. There was no hiding it anymore. I was compelled to

recite the numbers out loud. And if they did something wrong at the hospital, like someone dealt eight tiles instead of seven when playing Scrabble or an orderly delivered the evening meal late, I have to admit I'd get a little upset. And yell. A little bit. Throw things. Occasionally.

Over the next few weeks, as we tell our stories, it becomes obvious that the Germphobics are getting better. Edith, our star pupil, still has trouble touching things but it's not because of germs now. It's because she shakes a bit. Daria and Gemma are much better too. It turns out they are sisters who haven't spoken civilly for years. They were each suspicious that the other was only pretending to be obsessed, for a little sisterly fun. Soon Daria is going back to work as a podiatrist. Gemma still cries a bit during the sessions but now she's able to sleep at night without wrapping the bed in plastic.

Carla hasn't done so well. A few sessions later, Francine tells us she has dropped out. Francine says we shouldn't let Carla's disappearance disrupt our mental vision of a healthy and loving future. Gary is getting angrier as the sessions go on. He defends being a Germphobe on any level he can: intellectually, emotionally, even spiritually, because germs are still God's

creatures and Francine has no business denying their importance. I feel sorry for him. No job, no girlfriend, lives by himself—an empty life really. No wonder he needs his germs to keep him company.

Then, a week later, Francine vanishes for a while. By the time she gets off the penicillin drip and is out of the hospital, fully recovered from her gastro infection, Gary too is having second thoughts about his therapy. The rest of us wonder how long he'll last.

Seamus and I are at my place watching television. I watch television all day by myself, and at night with Seamus. After the morning show there's a cooking show featuring a hunky Greek-looking chef who seems very interested in talking to the cameraman. Next is some entertainment variety show, featuring stories about some starlet's mansion and another starlet's miracle inches-off Hollywood diet. Then various international soap operas (one featuring an evil twin who has been masquerading as his good brother and had fooled everyone, even his father, and another featuring an evil father who has been masquerading as his own good son to fool his evil brother) until a courtroom show, which is a kind of ritual humiliation of rednecks. Then another cooking show, this time with a bulbous chef who can't stop tasting everything. Then a kind of ritual humiliation of fat people, complete

with torture, which after a while I realize is a weight-loss show. Then a ritual humiliation of young, stupid, naked drunk people, a.k.a. a reality show. Then a ritual humiliation of greedy people, a.k.a. a quiz show. Then another soap opera.

Now we are watching two boys who were long-lost brothers discovering their supernatural powers, or something. The two brothers are handsome in that Hollywood way—even the compulsory ugly one would be, should you ever meet him in the flesh, actually the handsomest person you would ever see in your life. The same way American movies always cast a stunningly beautiful girl to play an ugly girl, and then give her one eyebrow, fluffy hair and glasses. This supernatural-brothers show is one of Seamus's favorites, but every night there seems to be one of his favorites, so we sit most nights silently for hours watching that glowing box in the corner. Tonight I can't really follow what's happening because my two brains are yabbering away (something about which of them is more beautiful, the physical brain or the thinking brain), so I try to smirk when Seamus does and groan when Seamus does. I catch his eye, but it takes a while to organize for the brains to make me smile. It's good to smile at him, though. Because sometimes when he catches my eye he looks a bit sad.

The phone rings.

Larry: Hello, Grace?

Brain Two: Thank God we're off that couch. Our arse has gone to sleep.

Brain One: If you would shut up I could follow the program. Now I'll never work out if the ex-girlfriend is a zombie.

Brain Two: Surely you can pick out a fellow zombie. Don't you guys have a secret handshake?

Larry: Grace, are you there?

Brain One: Hello. How are you?

Larry: Fine.

Brain One: How's the family?

Brain Two: I think she wants to talk about something else . . .

Brain One: That's good.

Larry: I didn't say anything.

Brain One: Good.

Larry: Mum says you're seeing a shrink.

Brain One: I'm fine, thanks. How are you?

Brain Two: Why are you seeing a shrink?

Larry: Well?

Brain One: Well what?

Larry: Are you seeing a shrink?

Brain Two: You're certainly not shrunk, anyway. Your arse is as big as a house.

Larry: Why are you laughing? What's funny?

Brain One: Nothing. Nothing's funny. I am seeing a highly recommended Professor Professor to help me build a staircase to a healthier future.

Larry: You sound different. I don't want you to change, Grace. I want you to be how you were before.

Brain One: I am how I was before. Only better. How are you?

Then Jill gets on the phone. I offer to babysit on the weekend so she and Harry can go out and have a romantic dinner. I feel more confident about getting around; I've taken the bus a few times and I'm getting quite good at it. And Larry is always asking me to visit. Jill says that sounds like a great idea, but then she checks with Larry. As Jill explains, kids Larry's age always have something on, and Larry has to go over to a girlfriend's place so it isn't convenient, and I'm not to take it personally. Which is okay.

Deciding on the holiday Seamus wants to take is hard too. I used to have a list of my ideal holiday spots, a list I'd had since I was a teenager that I'd taken from a travel magazine. San Sebastián, Spain. Lake Garda, Italy. Kenya. South Africa. Paris. London. I've never been to one of them. But now that it's time to plan a real holiday, I've lost all interest in my list. In fact, I

can't find it. I'm a bit blasé about the whole thing, if the truth be known. All that packing and unpacking. It hardly seems worth it. The other night I saw a fabulous documentary on the pyramids, and it was as good as being there, with no chance of traveler's tummy. No heat. No tourists. But I suppose it's good to get away. I'll just let Seamus choose.

Today I go for a walk in the park. It's growing colder and the leaves are starting to turn. There are lots of trees of all kinds, an old fountain and a greenhouse where plants accustomed to more consistent warmth than Melbourne provides have been grown for over a hundred years. There is a woman walking in front of me pushing a stroller. She stops next to a bench and sits her baby on her lap. The baby is in a yellow jumpsuit, the kind that encloses the feet. It is brushed cotton with small bluebirds embroidered near the shoulder. The woman holds the baby up so he is standing on his tippy toes and she is cooing, wrinkling up her nose and rubbing it against his squirming tummy.

I keep walking to the next bench, where I sit and pretend to admire the flowers. As the woman bounces the baby on her lap I can see their future: I can see him at three with sandy hair and a grazed knee, run-

ning to her and crying and her picking him up in her arms and burying his tears in her neck. I can see him at eight going to a football game with his hand in hers, clutching a flag and a pen, hoping for an autograph if they wait long enough, and they do because she knows how much it means to him and she is one of those patient women who will always have time for important things. At sixteen he goes through an awkward stage where he joins the chess club and decides to study law, but at twenty (after a year overseas in a youth exchange program where he loses his virginity to a Brazilian girl named Janis), he fills out and drops out to work part-time for Greenpeace and hand-make rustic wooden furniture using old timber he reclaims from demolished industrial buildings as a cross between art and protest.

Then it becomes a blur, a jumble of future memories—his first Christmas, fishing trips, his mother's days of burned toast and spilled tea, laughs and wrestles in the big bed, tears and tantrums at the checkout. His first wedding—to that woman who obviously isn't right for him but his mother doesn't say anything; she is just ready to hold him in her arms when the inevitable comes. The first time they watch *Seven Samurai* together. The first time he uses the potty. The day the dog dies and they bury it together, both crying

in the backyard, shovel in her hand, bunch of camellias in his. That tenderness that boys are made of before school and hormones frustrate and sharpen them. The warmth of a small child, freshly bathed and in his pajamas. The smell of a baby's neck.

The shadows in the park grow longer and the wind grows colder and when I look up they are gone. I am alone.

When I came to write about this in my journal— Francine says you can "write your way to a healthier you"—the best way I could describe my thoughts was this: When I was a small child my uncle gave me a kaleidoscope. As I turned the wheel the little glass chips jumped into webs and sunsets and necklaces. Thinking about that child in the park was like that, but with memories.

They love my journal in therapy, which is just as well because I feel hopelessly inadequate at conversation. They all speak so quickly that by the time the brains have decided what they want to say, everyone has moved on to another topic. My journal is clearly the best, though. The Germphobics are hopeless at journaling.

Francine: Sometimes it helps to greet your journal
 on each new day as you would greet a friend, so

your first line might be "Good morning, Journal. Thank you for accepting my words and feelings today."

Gemma: That is the most stupid concept I have ever heard. I would rather eat my own vomit than write greetings to a piece of paper.

Gary: There's nothing wrong with eating your own vomit.

Francine: What?

Gary: Eating your own vomit isn't actually disgusting. It's quite sensible really, because the germs present in your vomit are your own germs and you are merely reclaiming them rather than releasing them to the environment to infect someone else.

Daria: Gary, you are an idiot.

Francine: Well. Yes. This is a little off the track of this afternoon's session, which is journaling. Grace, would you like to read something from your journal?

Daria: Eating your own vomit is so absolutely disgusting, because obviously when you vomit it has to land somewhere unless you had a special kind of floating vomit, and once it lands it would then become contaminated from whatever it landed on, so if you eat it again you most certainly

ingest considerably more than your own germs back again.

Francine: Grace? Anyone?

Gary: Actually dogs eat their own vomit all the time.

Francine: What?

Gary: Dogs eat their own vomit all the time because they regurgitate anything that doesn't sit quite right in their stomach, but they don't want to waste it so they eat it again to see if it's any better the second time. And it usually is.

Gemma: It usually is what?

Gary: A substantial improvement. The second time.

Francine: Grace, can you read your journal please? Now?

Journal: Autumn is now officially half over. The tree outside my window has lost most of its leaves. In spring, new growth will bring new life.

Francine: Beautiful, Grace! What a touching analogy of your healing process!

Brain One: I knew that. Really. I did.

Brain Two: You are so full of crap.

Journal: Therapy is progressing well, but I haven't yet received a bill. I know the bills will come,

because I have filled out the forms. I know I can pay them, and I know my sister will help. Yet I still haven't received a bill.

Francine: Oh, Grace, dear Grace. Yes, you may not contribute very much to our group discussions but rest assured, you pay your bills every session! When you listen so attentively to your fellow group members speak. When you concentrate so hard on not counting. I'm glad you shared your fears, but please don't think like that. Every day, you face your bills. And every day, brave, brave Grace, you pay them.

Brain One: Um . . . thanks.

Brain Two: I'm disgusted to be sharing a skull with you.

Journal: Before my therapy, each night I cooked chicken and vegetables. And I ate it. Alone. Now, although I am always hungry, I have lost the will to cook. Now I make cheese on toast, or dip with crackers or chocolate cookies. Or I buy a burger from the café.

Daria: I don't believe you used to eat chicken.

Gemma: That is so disgusting. How can you live with yourself?

Brain One: What's wrong with chicken?

Daria: Don't you read the papers?

Gemma: Haven't you ever heard of bird flu?

Daria: I don't even go out of the house if there's a pigeon on the lawn.

Francine: Ladies, I think you'll find that Grace is making an analogy about the changes she has experienced in the way she feeds her body—her psychic and emotional hunger for validation and acceptance.

Brain One: Absolutely.

Brain Two: I can't take this anymore. I'm having a nap. Wake me when it's lunchtime.

Chapter 14

Seamus and I are almost living together now. He still has his room in the house he shares with Dermot and Brian, but it's a bachelor pad—dirty dishes in the sink, dirty clothes on the floor and someone always sprawled on the couch watching sports. We end up spending most of our time at my place. Seamus keeps his running shoes and his toothbrush here, and I buy the kind of cereal he likes.

It's much easier for me this way, because I'd worry about forgetting my medication if I wasn't sure which house I was waking up in. Also it's much easier for me to get to the professor's office from my place than from Seamus's. I catch the tram, by myself. I'm only seeing the professor once a month now to check how the medication and therapy are going. I miss him. I saw a furry

caterpillar in the park last week and thought fondly of his eyebrows.

One morning I had a few jobs to do—drop off Seamus's dry cleaning, take his shoes to be repaired, pay the electricity bill. Then there was a fascinating show on TV about gay men trapped in women's bodies and lesbians trapped in men's bodies. A psychologist (not mine) was saying it was very common; many men are lesbians on the inside. I'd never realized the pain these people go through—I've been horribly insensitive to male lesbians.

I've given up going to the café. With all the extra weight I'm carrying there is no way I could have orange cake and a hot chocolate every day. Instead I make myself some carrot sticks and one and a half dates with tahini, which is much less nauseating now that I'm used to it. A couple of days ago I phoned my mother and we had a lovely chat about housework. I've kept everything clean in the past, but I'd never really grasped the finer details. We talked about the best ways to fold fitted sheets (hold the sheet inside out by the two adjacent corners on the shortest end, then fold the corner in one hand over the corner in the other end until it envelops it, then repeat with the other side), and the correct way to iron tea towels and shirts. I've never realized how clever she is. For example, when I iron Seamus's shirts I always do the collar last. This inevita-

bly leads to the front creasing. Instead I should iron the inside of the collar first. Genius! Then we talked about which TV chefs we liked the best. We both agreed that Ainsley gives us a headache, and Delia, while she explains things clearly in a charming accent, is a teeny bit annoying. Then my mother said that Jamie made her want to play hide the cannelloni. I felt suddenly nauseous so I said good night.

I'm glad my phone conversations are improving. It's hard for the brains to concentrate on what the ears are hearing. For once I raised it as an issue in group therapy sessions and felt so validated when two of the Germphobics nodded. Francine had a few helpful suggestions and I follow her advice to keep a box of index cards by the phone, filled with the details of the people I speak to. There are only four cards but when I get a job I'm sure there'll be more. For example, card one:

NAME: Seamus Joseph O'Reilly
RELATIONSHIP: Boyfriend
DOB: January 5, 1969
SIGNIFICANT NAMES: Declan, Dermot, Brian, Kylie
COMMENTS: [space here for comments]

Under "Comments" I write a sentence to remind me of our last phone call, like "picking me up 9 A.M. Saturday." This has proved so helpful it's a wonder I

haven't seen it on *Oprah*. I also keep an exercise book and when I have a few minutes to spare I plan the next conversation I will have with someone. For example, under "Neighbors" I have written "Comment on flowering azalea in front garden." Of course I don't have the book with me when I run into the neighbors in the corridor, but it's still helpful. I can't imagine how I did without it all these years.

There is no good whatsoever to be had from a phone call in the middle of the night. At no time in the history of mankind has anyone rung at that hour smiling. There are no lotteries drawn in foreign countries that you might have won. There are no exciting job offers made by insomniac managing directors of huge multinationals. Distant men do not propose at that hour. There is not even any so-so news. No telemarketer from Delhi desperate to talk about your phone contract. No partner asking you to pick up more juice.

The night the phone rings at some ungodly hour, I can't seem to wake up. I can hear a distant pealing but it's ingrained in my dream.

In the dream I'm relaxing at home in the early afternoon watching *Oprah* when the doorbell rings. This is, for some reason, alarming. I jump up almost

screaming. Who is at the door? Have they come to get me? What will Seamus think?

In a panic, I run to the window, which is somehow on the ground floor, and jump out. I try to run but my bathrobe keeps wrapping around my ankles and my slippers are flopping sideways. Whoever is at the door is chasing me, gaining on me, I can feel their breath on my neck; they are coming now and no matter how hard I try I can't get away. I fall and am pounced upon by a midget policeman.

For his size, the midget policeman is strong and wiry. He has a red beard and wears a green police uniform. "We've got you now," he keeps yelling, and laughs in a high-pitched voice. He hauls me to my feet and twists my arms behind my back, fastening them in a pair of handcuffs. Then he attaches heavy iron manacles to my ankles. My limbs are thus pinned and as he drags me down the path I can only take tiny steps, but he walks faster and pulls me by my arm until I am walking on an angle so steep I feel I am falling. Perhaps this is all a dream, I think to myself, and I shut my eyes. But then I can't open them again. They seem welded shut. Then I realize the sound of his laughter has morphed into the ringing of the phone.

Seamus leans over me in bed and answers it, making serious, capable noises into the receiver. Noises that

betray nothing. Seamus has the ability to be instantly alert at any time of the day or night; I seem to be sleepy all the time lately, and now I can't wake up properly. My eyelids are fused together, and I can only open one at a time and then only a little bit. My brains aren't helping—you would think the two of them could make each other a cup of coffee or something. By the time Brain One asks Brain Two to open my right eye or lift my left arm and put it through the sleeve, Brain Two has slumped to the floor of the red padded room and nodded off. When it doesn't receive a reply, Brain One becomes so disgruntled it also falls straight back to sleep.

Before I know it Seamus is up, changed into jeans and a sweatshirt. He gathers my tracksuit and lifts my jammies (mauve baby-doll type that were probably sexy when he bought them but are now, well, a little tight) up over my outstretched arms and dresses me. He practically carries me to the car. When I wake up we are in a parking lot.

It isn't until we are in the hospital waiting room that I really comprehend what has happened. Jill is there, also in a tracksuit, although hers is a crushed cranberry velour instead of a stained and stretched pastel blue like mine. Still, I never imagined she would even own a tracksuit. She certainly would never sweat. I've never

seen her hair like this either—dead straight instead of
her usual curls. Obviously the result of a silk pillow-
case. I must get one. She is not wearing makeup and
her eyes look tiny and pale like pig eyes, and she has
brown spots along her jawline.

Harry is there too, wearing a pinstriped navy suit
and turquoise tie, as if it was early afternoon. Perhaps
he's just arrived home from a midnight board meeting.
Or perhaps he sleeps in his suit for improved efficiency.
Or it isn't a suit, but jammies designed to look like a
suit, sold by mail order from Suitland. Or (my pre-
ferred explanation) perhaps he has no option because
the suit has been surgically attached to his skin as part
of a bizarre initiation ceremony at the bank involving
donkeys and paddles.

Hospitals have an unearthly feeling at that hour.
This is a public hospital, not far from our mother's
house, the one we grew up in, the one that we moved
to when I was at primary school. The waiting room has
plastic orange chairs against the walls and in an island
in the middle. The chairs are in rows, joined together
to prevent people from moving, throwing or stealing
them. The chairs hold an assortment of people waiting
to be seen, though some of them are lying down and
groaning. The Germphobics would be spraying each
other with disinfectant and praying for levitation.

Jill and Harry haven't met Seamus before and, except for the obviously horrible circumstances, it is an ideal occasion for a first meeting. No diffidence. No awkwardness. Plenty to talk about—three take-charge kind of people discussing options and possibilities. I sit next to a nice Somali boy who can't move his storm-cloud-colored sausage-shaped fingers after drunkenly punching an automatic teller machine that swallowed his card. I have a little doze on his other shoulder.

Seamus wakes me. There's a nurse, saying something.

She is all right, the nurse says. She has some smoke inhalation and some minor burns and was distressed when the ambulance brought her in, but they've given her a mild sedative and she's sleeping now. They'll keep her in for observation and to check her lung function during the night, but overall she is very lucky. Sophie the next-door neighbor saw the smoke, and her son put out the fire with the garden hose before the brigade even arrived. The fireman told the nurse that the damage to the house is also minimal and with some fast work from a few tradesmen it will be functional at least when she gets out of the hospital. Sophie was most insistent Mother be told that Mr. Parker is okay.

Jill storms across to the far side of the waiting room and back again. She riffles in her handbag for some

gum, and throws her bag on the chair, and says she blames herself and that Mother shouldn't be living alone in that big house and should have moved in with them long ago. Harry clears his throat and fiddles with his tie, pulling it away slightly from his reddening, chicken-skin throat. (If his suit is attached to his body, the stitches obviously aren't at the neck. Are they at the groin?)

The nurse says it's nobody's fault. These things happen with older people and there's not much you can do. Jill says what on earth did happen? The nurse says, from what I could gather before your mother became too drowsy to speak, apparently she couldn't sleep and she was hungry and decided to make herself a midnight snack. A frozen chicken Kiev. She read the instructions on the packet very carefully. It said medium oven, forty minutes. And she only put it on for thirty. But she didn't want to go to all the trouble of lighting the oven so she popped the whole thing, chicken, foil tray, cardboard box and all, in the microwave.

A little later they let us in to see Mother. She is in a large room with four beds, but hers is the only one occupied. We aren't to stay long. We aren't to disturb her. She is sleeping, so we stand around her bed, looking her, not quite knowing what to say to each oth

Her face is the same color as the sheets, a dingy gray; her hair is pushed straight back and one hand is bandaged above the wrist. She looks deflated. Normally she is like a fat-faced bird, a cross between Céline Dion and a cockatoo: a body like a broom handle and round cheeks full of seeds. Now it's like the seeds have all fallen out. It's strange to see her face so immobile—not speaking, grimacing or sucking her teeth, which she does when she's concentrating or telling a cheerful story about dying in an unexpected and painful way.

For some reason I think of the birthday presents she gave me as a child. She was the most wonderful gift giver when I was small—it seemed that whatever my most secret wish, there it was, beautifully wrapped at the end of my bed on the morning of my birthday. Once she gave me a huge cardboard box covered in brown paper with a stiff iridescent gold bow. The box was so large and heavy she left it in the middle of the living room where she wrapped it the night before. In the morning when I tore the paper away, it was full of books. She isn't much of a reader except for true crime, gothic horror and (probably the most gruesome of the three) tabloid newspapers, but, on advice from a confident and superior sales assistant, she chose my first Austen and Conan Doyle, my first Poe and Wilde.

Another year she promised me a new bedspread and took me to choose it the week before, but then told me the store had sold out so it wouldn't be ready for my birthday. I don't recall being upset, but perhaps my memory is being kind. I think I was only a little disappointed for her: it wasn't her fault the shop was out of stock and I had to wait. So that birthday morning there was no gift from my parents, only a beaded bracelet from Jill.

When I got home from school, not only was the bedspread on my bed, but she had taken a day off work and now my room, the walls, even the ceiling, were repainted my favorite color: the orange I always called tan, an exact match for Cuisenaire rod number 10. There was a new tan chair, a new bed and a shiny tan lampshade that cast the whole room in a rosy orange glow. I still don't know how she found that perfect color. That day, standing in the hall next to my mother, her pudgy arms shaking from painting the ceiling and her face speckled tan, was possibly the happiest of my life.

Now Jill, Seamus and Harry are murmuring, and I force myself to pay attention. It'll be much better for her, Harry says. These stubborn old people, they never think of anyone but themselves. Jill says, anything could happen to her, she could take a fall and lie there

all day and all night. My granny loved it, Seamus says, once we got her settled she made lots of new friends now someone comes in to do her hair and they play bingo. Good man, Harry says. You're absolutely right it's for her own good and she can always watch TV besides she'll be happier among other old people.

Then he says, there's safety in numbers.

Somewhere inside me something stirs. I can't explain it. A little voice speaks. It isn't Brain One or Brain Two. Perhaps it's me.

"A home," I say. "You're talking about putting her in a nursing home."

Harry laughs and Jill says yes Grace yes we're talking about putting her in a home it's obvious she can't live alone anymore.

"Mother would hate that."

Jill walks over to me and picks up my hand and holds it and says, we don't have many options Grace think of how we'd feel if she stayed at home and had an accident think how you'd feel then.

"But she loves her neighbors and the church and her garden. You know how much that house means to her."

It happens to the best of us, Harry says, it'll happen to us one day too, hey Jilly besides Grace you heard what Seamus said they have hairdressers and bingo.

Bingo. Those little cards. Those funny press-down pens.

All those numbers.

Mother is lying in the bed right in front of us while we are speaking about her. Ants. They want to turn her into an ant. When I was teaching those fiery little minds, I knew they would eventually be worn down by the drudgery and disappointments of life. Ants. They would all become average, huddling little ants, indistinguishable and unremarkable. And when they were no longer useful they would live in a garbage dump filled with other ants. Staring at the walls. Their belongings, gathered with so much care, would scatter. Will scatter. They will cease. My mother will cease.

She's mumbling, Harry says. Grace?

"She doesn't like bingo," I say. "She loves her house. What about Mr. Parker? What about all her orchids?"

Harry says what? What did you say? I can't understand her.

Jill says Grace our mother could have died that's all that matters we can find another home for Mr. Parker and the orchids don't even flower nursing homes have gardens too you know some of them even have cats the most important thing is she'll be safe.

I force my eyes to stay open. I force my mouth to move. "Safe. That house has been her home for years,"

I say. "She has lived a life there. With her husband and her children. She's a grown woman. It should be up to her if she stays or if she goes."

Jill sighs. It's a hard decision for us all Grace I understand that you don't want to see her institutionalized after your experience the year before last but we can't look after her we can't keep her safe in a home she'll have doctors and nurses and support and medication and she'll be safe I thought you would understand that you of all people with what you've gone through lately.

Harry says, I hope you're not suggesting we put her up we've got three kids you know she can't have my study.

The ground tilts and I reach out for Seamus's arm. My tongue has gone to sleep and my mouth seems to be full of treacle. "We haven't even asked her. She's healthy. She's active. We could make it easier for her to stay."

Seamus says, sweetie your sister is right it's for the best.

I am unbearably tired. My right eye is closing and I can't stop it.

Everyone wants what's best for her sweetheart, Seamus says, this is all overwhelming and it's late and the shock's probably been too much for you you should probably try to have a rest.

He takes my arm and walks me to a corner of the room where there is an orange plastic chair, like the ones in the waiting room but a single. He stands in front of me with both hands around my upper arms and slowly sits me down. I sag into the chair, my head lolling.

Relax sweetheart just sit here and relax while we discuss it.

So the three of them go on discussing it. And me.

Harry says, God Jill she's always been a bit odd but I can barely understand her. Seamus says, it's not her fault it's the medication there's been a few side effects so they've started her on another kind her doctor says this is the transition period she'll feel better in a few days God she's been so brave I never imagined it would change her so much. Jill says, is there anything we can do to help her? Seamus says, she doesn't seem to want to talk about it I'd do anything to help her but I don't know what to do. Jill says, I know she'd never say it but she loves Mum very much so do we all it'll be much better when Mum is somewhere she'll be looked after. Harry says, actually, does your mother have any money? Your father's insurance was quite a packet wasn't it?

They're probably right. I should let them handle it. I open my eyes a sliver and in her bed I see Mother turning her head from side to side. Perhaps she can hear us

after all. Perhaps she can hear every word about packing her away in a nursing home. Could they not stop talking and let her sleep? Let me sleep. I am so tired. Please let me crawl in next to Mother in her hospital bed and put my head on her shoulder and have a little nap.

Harry, Jill and Seamus stand together in a triangle speaking in loud whispers. From the slit between my eyelids I can see the three of them, arms crossed in exactly the same fashion—left over right. Peas in a pod. I try to focus and listen. I close my eyes again, and snippets of their words float past. Mum's always been unlucky . . . accident prone . . . just as well there are no stairs in that house.

Seamus says, Grace told me all about the accident when you were kids did you and Grace get another puppy when you moved to this house I mean.

"Puppy?" Jill says. "Mum's always been a cat person. We never had a puppy."

Chapter 15

It's nearly dawn when we get home. Even in the car I can't stay awake. I am dozing on and off but Seamus doesn't say anything. Not one word.

When we pull up he jumps out and comes around to my side and helps me out. He still doesn't speak. He takes my keys from my fingers and opens the security door. Not one word, up the stairs or as he opens my door.

He helps me out of my clothes and into my pajamas, the reverse of a few hours ago. He brings me a glass of water and puts my slippers next to the bed. He tucks me in, squeezing the sheet and the blanket so tightly under the edge of the mattress that my arms and legs are pinned. I can hear him sigh and feel him sit down beside me. His weight is heavy on the edge of

the mattress, dragging me down so steeply that for a moment I feel I am falling. My eyelids are glued shut.

Seamus says, "I know you can hear me, Grace."

There is a silence.

"There was no puppy," he says. "Was there, Grace?"

I dig my fingernails into my palms. I open my eyes and stare straight at him.

"No. No, there was no puppy."

He leans toward me, one arm resting on the bed on the other side of my body. "What did happen on the back stairs?"

I feel a wetness on my palms. My nails have drawn blood. "It was an accident. Exactly how I told you, except it was my brother. My baby brother Daniel fell down the stairs."

He stands up and walks to the door, head in his hands. He comes back and kneels beside the bed so his face is level with mine.

"I'm so sorry, Grace. I didn't realize."

I think of all the small acts of love he has given me. The wonderful sex where he cares as much for my pleasure as his own. How I felt more alive naked with him than I have ever felt before. Reading the papers in bed on a Sunday morning. His kisses on the small of my back. Laughing in the park, when he told me

something he had heard on the radio. Cooking me spaghetti when I was tired. The way he could eat chili like his mouth was made of asbestos. The two of us, under the shower.

And all this time he thought I was someone else. "Well, you do now. Now you know exactly what kind of a person I am."

He reaches out and tries to touch my face. I turn away. "It doesn't change anything," he says.

My mouth is so dry I can barely speak. "Bullshit. It changes everything."

"No, Grace. It doesn't. The only thing that matters is why you lied to me."

I try to laugh. "Why didn't I casually mention on our first date that I killed my baby brother? I can't imagine."

"Since then, I mean. I've never felt as close to anyone as I feel to you. For God's sake, Grace. You were just a kid. It was an accident. Why didn't you trust me?"

I can't feel my palms anymore, so I dig my nails into my thighs. I can do this.

"So this is all about you, now, is it? About poor Seamus, whose girlfriend didn't tell him the truth. News flash, Seamus: it's not about you. It's about me."

He tenses his jaw. "I hoped it might be about us."

"Well it's not. For fuck's sake, grow up. You don't own me, or my mind or my memory. I owe you nothing."

His hand forms a fist, and he holds it in front of his mouth. "Maybe we shouldn't talk now. The shock of your mother's accident. The medication . . . you're saying things you don't mean."

"I know exactly what I mean. I've been meaning to say it for ages."

He turns his head away.

"I'm sick to death of you, you self-righteous, controlling shit. I'm sick of being judged by you. I am. God, I'm so sick of sitting there watching TV. I want to be myself again. No, don't touch me. Just get out."

He doesn't move.

"Get out," I say. "I mean it."

"Think about what you're saying, Grace. Please."

"I've thought about nothing else for weeks. Find someone else to rescue, you average, average man. There's nothing wrong with me."

Those final words exhaust me. I can't manage any more. For such a long time I've been so tired. Now I am finally lying in my bed, all tucked in. I can sleep for as long as I want. For weeks. For years.

I feel the bed move as he stands up. I feel him walk away and hear him pick up his keys and cross the room. I hear the front door shut. Then my eyes open wide.

I can't keep them shut. Can't sleep after all. So I lie there, still as a corpse.

And I think. I think about a lot of things. About my mother and her house and her cat and her orchids. About our phone conversations every Sunday night. About how she painted my room, still a faded, peeling tan, now full of her gardening books. About nursing homes. All her meals would be cooked for her so there was no risk of burning the house down. No midnight snacks. No housework to do. No sheets to wash and iron and fold.

I look down the length of the bed. Under the quilt are the larger-than-expected mounds of a torso and two legs. I think about that body lying there, plump and flabby, under the covers; the same body I see every morning in the bathroom mirror. I wonder whose it is. It doesn't look like Jill's or Larry's. But it can't be mine.

I think about my two brains, thankfully sleeping. They are lying on the floor of the red padded room in their matching red jammies in each other's arms. At least they've made up from their most recent squabble. I think about where they came from and where they might go after I finish with them.

I think about how long it is since I've spoken with Larry, what it would be like growing up with Jill and Harry as parents. I think about Francine; good, kind, helpful Francine. And the Germphobics, most of whom, everyone agrees, are getting better.

I think about babies. How beautiful they are. How soft. How so many women I see in the street and at the shopping center seem to be at ease with them, as if it was completely ordinary for a woman to have a baby. How babies are brand new, and to have one would almost be like starting life over. Getting another chance to make things right.

I think about what Harry said. It was possibly the only true thing he has ever said: "There's safety in numbers."

I look around my bedroom. It is mind-numbingly ordered. It looks like an Ikea catalog. The walls are white. Plain. No numbers. The drawers of my repainted dresser obviously hold clothes. So does my wardrobe. I have no idea how many.

On the bedside table, still in its silver frame, is that photo of the dead inventor. He has a face that seems out of time, as if there is no way that face could be alive now. His eyebrows are on a jaunty angle and his mustache is freshly preened. He is looking right at me with an insolent kind of dare in his gaze. He's daring me.

I look at the digital clock by the bed, the only remaining numbers in my whole life. The green glowing lines say 5:55 A.M.

It is time to get up.

Chapter 16

When a grown woman wearing stretched mauve baby-doll pajamas and matching fluffy slippers and carrying a portable television knocks on your door at 6:05 A.M., I suppose it might be slightly disconcerting. At least the 5 Indian students in the flat downstairs seem to think so when they answer, rubbing their eyes, in their grimy T-shirts and Y-fronts. They wake up quickly enough when I give them the TV. (I did consider tossing it out the window—more rock star, less World Vision.) Their own set died 4 months ago and is in the corner of the room in 17 pieces. They shake their 5 heads in unison. No, they couldn't possibly. Surely I will need it. You can't live without a television. Besides, it's almost brand new. Finally one brave soul says yes, and then they all laugh.

"Is there anything we can do for you, madam?" the tall one asks. "In return for your kindness?"

"Now that you mention it, there is," I reply. "Could you nip down to the post office this afternoon? And would you have a spare cardboard box?"

When you phone the aged care division of the Department of Human Services, especially at 1 minute past 9 in the morning, they can organize things at a clip. First, an appointment for mother with an aged care assessment team. Then, based on the results, Meals on Wheels three times a week consisting of soup, a main course and dessert. Most geriatrics eat the soup for lunch (reduces unnecessary daytime chewing) and the entrée and dessert for dinner (reduces unnecessary nighttime fires). Day trips once a week, so she can get out and meet new old people. Even a cleaner, not that she needs one. It turns out there's a raft of services designed to keep the oldies out of expensive nursing homes. It's also a good idea, they said, to replace the gas oven with electric so it's easier to use and she won't be tempted to misuse the microwave.

When white pills—when 22 little white pills—hit the toilet bowl, they float. They bob up and down like Francine's apple would have. Unlike Francine, I have no desire to pluck them out and eat them. When I push the button, they hesitate for a moment then huddle

together in a paroxysm of fear. They shudder. They're going down! Bracing themselves, they hurl violently clockwise before disappearing in a scream and a gurgle. I suck in my tummy (what a pointless gesture) to give the illusion of military pomp and offer a final salute. 'Tis a far, far better thing, etc.

The cardboard box I place in the middle of the living room. Then, in a rotating arc starting from the north I open every cupboard and drawer and scan every hidden spot. As I find each foreign thing—a toothbrush that isn't one of mine, running shoes and 2 pairs of socks, a box of cereal that's too sweet, a jar of Asian chili paste, a navy blue baseball cap, sunglasses, a packet of supermarket safety razors, DVDs of *Mulholland Drive* and *The Sopranos* series 3—I place it in the box in the exact position it was found, as if the box was a scaled-down apartment. Then I fill the box with newspaper, scrunched so that nothing will move in transit. I seal it with duct tape over and over and write the contents on one side and the address on the other. Even thus entombed I can't touch it. I yell over the railing and the Indian boys come upstairs and pick it up.

When a significantly overweight, terminally unemployed, friendless, recently frigid, probably eternally childless spinster phones to cancel her therapy, some

questions will be asked. I leave these calls for a day or so to make sure my strength is up.

"Well, I'm astonished!" Francine says. "I thought you were going to make it, Grace! Are you sure I can't convince you to change your mind?"

"Francine, therapy has taught me many things. The first is this: life is like a bunch of flowers."

"Yes?"

"Not a bunch of roses, not a bunch of lilies. A mixed bunch."

"Yes, yes?"

"Different flowers bloom at different times, Francine. When the rose is full and red, the carnation is beginning to open. When the petals of the lily are shriveling and dropping that annoying orange dust all over the hall table, the gerbera is still perfect. Often because it has a wire stuck up its stem. I understand this now, deep within myself, and I have you to thank."

"Oh, Grace. That's beautiful. You're very welcome. And remember, when your carnation is ready to open, we'll be here."

Professor Segrove is more circumspect. "Well, it's your decision of course, but we were making so much progress. You were more than halfway up the staircase."

"And I'm sure the view from the top is magnificent. But I've decided I prefer both feet on the ground."

Harrumph. "Grace, please make sure when you come off the medication you taper the dose to minimize withdrawal symptoms."

Memo to self: when next considering coming off antidepressants cold turkey, choose something easier instead like teaching a Big Brother housemate advanced trigonometry. I spend the next 2 weeks feeling as if my brains are renovating. I can see them in their little matching pink overalls, dust masks and earmuffs, pulling out cabinetry and slamming sledgehammers through drywall. I wish they would take more care. For all they know some of those walls could be structural.

During those first 2 weeks, the phone rings and rings. 5 times on Monday. 5 times on Tuesday. 8 times on Wednesday. Twice on Friday and twice on Saturday. On Saturday, there is also some insistent knocking on the door. And again on Sunday. I lean with my back against the door so I can feel the knocks through my body. On Sunday night, at 8:00 and 8:20, I take the calls. Mother (still slightly hoarse) and Jill, trained like Labradors. The phone rings again the following Wednesday. When the phone's not ringing, my life is silent. I walk to the kitchen to tell Seamus something, but he's not there. By the third week, except for Mother and Jill, the phone doesn't ring at all.

It requires some time to get back to my routine. Obviously I need a new café, but in Glen Iris there are more cafés than people. What is everyone doing in cafés all day? Not much farther than the old one, but in the opposite direction, is a café I like just fine. No Monet prints; instead violently colored artworks by local students. No annoying Cheryl; instead bustling teenage girls and a barista named Roberto.

It takes some time to catalog all my belongings again, but this time I count everything. Not just clothes and plates and books, but cotton balls, paper clips, tea bags. I measure all the walls anew and record them in my replacement notebook. I work fast. The streets surrounding my flat I capture again in paces and—an innovation long overdue—one morning as the sun is rising I count and measure in height and width all the plants in the front garden of my block. I cannot yet take the length and circumference of my digits, limbs and torso, because they are still not mine. Every surface he has touched is scrubbed. The sheets and towels I throw away and replace by mail order.

On the Saturday of the fourth week after I finished therapy, it's freezing outside so I delay the walk home by reading the entire paper (allowed in extreme weather conditions). Why is Saturday's paper so big? Who buys

all these houses? Who reads all these columns? And who on earth cares about all these actors?

I'm flicking mindlessly through the employment pages when in the corner I see a small ad pressed between "Executive Assistants" and "Customer Service Operators." Part-time data-entry operator, it says. Work from home. Set your own hours—telecommute! It's the workforce of the future! Beat the traffic! Casual rates (no holiday pay, pension, sick leave, parental leave, compassionate leave or any other benefits whatsoever) apply.

In my hurry to rip the ad out I almost spill my chocolate. I could do this. I could work from home. I could plan a schedule and work, say, 8:30 to 10:00 A.M. Then walk to the coffee shop. Then I'd start again at 10:45. I could organize my day exactly as I want. I could work out a certain number of pages to enter each, say, half-hour block. I could count something . . . anything . . . keystrokes or sheets or whatever. I can do this. I pick up my jacket and pay Roberto. It's time to dare the weather, go home and fabricate a CV.

In the weeks that follow, I spend a lot of time talking with Mother. She's fully recovered with lots of new potted plants to tend—get-well gifts from the congregation. I've told her the plan to help her stay in the house and it's working already. I've briefed her

on what to say to Jill if she mentions a nursing home. It's our own little conspiracy. I let her get settled again first, but eventually I have to tell her.

"Mum, I've been meaning to talk to you about something. It's Seamus. I . . . we broke up."

She inhales sharply, a sound I mistake for shock. "And who was Seamus again, dear?"

"He was my boyfriend. You remember. The Irish one? The one who wasn't a comedian or a terrorist?"

The breath comes out again, an old-lady sigh. "Oh yes, of course. I remember now. Well, well, dear. Have you decided you prefer girls?"

This time the inhalation is mine, even sharper. "What?" How does she even know about that? I'm pretty sure it wasn't invented in her day.

"I was just wondering if you broke up with that Irish boy because you've decided you prefer girls. It seems to be so popular nowadays. Perhaps that's the reason you haven't been very successful with men. After all, you're so pretty and funny and bright."

I think of whiskers that catch under my nail when I jag my finger along a jaw. The cleft at the base of a throat, underneath the Adam's apple. Chest hair tinged with gray. The lines of muscle along a shoulder blade.

"Thanks for asking, Mum, but I don't think I prefer girls."

"You should be beating them off with a stick, dear. I wish your father could see you. He'd be very proud."

For a minute, I do no breathing at all.

"I wish Dad were here too."

"Well, I still want you to be careful."

The conversation is back on track. Impending disaster. Good. "Careful of what, Mum?"

"Remember what happened to that nice Anne Heche when she split up with Ellen DeGeneres? She had a breakdown and then wrote that book where she said she was sexually abused by her father and she was the daughter of God and the half sister of Jesus and she spoke to little green men from outer space. And she made that movie where she had to kiss Harrison Ford and he was old enough to be her grandfather. It was very unsavory. That kind of thing is enough to warp young minds."

I consider my mother many things, but not a bigot.

"What are you saying, Mum? That lesbians are crazy? That gay women can warp young minds?"

"Oh no, dear. Kissing your grandfather can warp young minds. Don't tell anyone at the church this, but I think girls going out with girls is quite sensible. Imagine not having to do all the housework, and if you found a nice girl the same size you'd have double the wardrobe and you'd never have to shave your legs or clean

whiskers out of the sink. I don't know why everyone doesn't do it. No, it's fine, provided you stay that way. It's the changing back to men that sends you mad."

It's times like this (speaking to my mother on the phone) that I really miss my 2 brains, even though they were incredibly rude after all the hospitality I'd shown them. They didn't even say good-bye. I didn't notice them packing—no matching capillary-pink plaid suitcases, no neuron-gray duffel bags. One morning I woke up and they were gone.

Another morning I wake up and have to work out a new cleaning regime, and a new morning regime and a new nighttime regime. And a new dinner regime, with new food (a complex, revolving menu taken from the recipes in the newspaper) because I can't stomach either chicken with vegetables or cheese on toast any-more. And I love my new café; they fill me with con-fidence. For a start, they don't have orange cake every day—their cakes have more variety and are fresher. They even have real maple syrup for their pancakes, unlike the toxic waste they gave me at the last place that day I had breakfast with Seamus. The first morn-ing we woke up together.

I've refined and improved lots of things: for instance, I'm now starting with the cake that's in the top left-hand corner of the display case and moving one cake to the

left every day. I like this much more—it's a better fit to my usual habit of clockwise table rotation. And it's the number of words the teenage waitress says when she greets me that determines the number of bites. "Good morning! How are you today? Which cake would you like?" is 11, but it's amazing the variations she comes up with, including "I like your skirt," "I'd better write this down 'cause I'm a bit hungover" and "I'd give the eggs a miss today if I were you." This is much more fun than poppy seeds because I have to pay enough attention to respond naturally while counting at the same time.

I've found a new supermarket too: again, not much farther but in a rival chain. I choose the busiest night, Sunday, to pace it out. It's less conspicuous than counting steps in an empty store with the staff staring and deciding whether to call security, but you mustn't be waylaid by errant children and men staring aimlessly at the shelves. All my essentials are there and there's even a new size of Ziploc bag. Extra small. Perfect for my new afternoon snack of 10 almonds.

The same week I tell Mother, I decide to level with Jill. Sunday night, 18 degrees. I've been carefully avoiding the topic of Seamus and my therapy. But I can't put it off any longer and just when I thought nothing could take me unawares, Jill leaves me hanging on the phone, stunned.

"Can't say I'm surprised."

"You're not surprised I stopped therapy?"

"Of course not. It was never your kind of thing. We all have problems, you know, Grace. Every one of us. Harry . . . Harry, don't play with your football inside, please, darling."

I loathe the way parents think they are so bloody indispensable. They never give you their full attention in person, either. Always one eye, one ear and half a brain on the bloody kids. Once you're a parent, you sign away part of your brain forever.

"And also . . . I've broken up with Seamus."

"Not surprised about that either."

This is really too much. I was expecting shrieking, crying and an insistence that I have ruined my life. "Why? What was wrong with him?"

"Nothing. Look, Grace, I really liked him. I thought he was a catch. But he wasn't right for you."

"Why on earth wasn't he right for me?"

"I don't know exactly how to say this. He was a lovely man, but . . . you've always hated people like him. Average people with average jobs. Ordinary looks. Average house in an average suburb. I suppose he was tall but that was really his only distinguishing feature. Remember what you used to say about the ants? 'Racing in lines across my balcony as the sun is rising only to race back the other way as it sets.' Grace? Are you still there?"

Still here.

"I'm not saying I didn't like him. I did. But he was average. That's all."

She can talk. She's stuck in wedded purgatory with that BlackBerry-wielding ferret. He's got the sex appeal of a hard drive. Seamus was hot. Jill wouldn't know hot if she backed into it naked in the shower.

I've twirled my fingers through the phone cord and it takes me 10 seconds to get them out. "Larry liked Seamus too, right?"

"We all did. Actually Hilly's been a bit upset lately. She's worried about you, Grace. She said the therapy was turning you into a . . . I think she said 'tosser.' "

"Can I talk to her?"

"Hilly! Your auntie Grace is on the phone." There's some rustling and pretty soon . . .

"Hello?" Her voice is small. Did she always sound this tentative?

"Thanks for nothing." Larry in that house with her brother, sister and parents reminds me of a tiny gladiator surrounded by lions. It's so good to hear her voice; it's hard to even pretend to be cross.

"What? What did I do?" I imagine her mouth in a pout.

"Your mother says you thought I was turning into a tosser."

She's thinking that all adults are the same and she always seems to be in trouble and life is not fair and when she grows up she will move to Mars and never speak to any of us again. "Great. Thanks a lot, Mum."

"So why didn't you say something? We're supposed to be friends."

I can hear squeaking, and Jill in the background. "For heaven's sake, Hilly, lift that stool—don't drag it. You're leaving marks on the parquetry."

"I dunno . . . Dad said it was good. They were going to make you more normal."

"Normal shnormal. I dropped out."

"Oh."

"This is so typical of you. I remember when I got that perm and I thought it looked fantastic. Did you say anything? No. I looked hideous, I looked like a white chick pretending to be a black chick and did you tell me it looked awful? Did you tell me I'd look better bald? No. So thanks for nothing."

She thinks hard. "What perm? When was this?"

"1985 of course. When else would I have had a perm? I was trying to look like Madonna. In her perm period."

"Der. I wasn't born then."

"Typical bloody excuse. You are supposed to be my friend. You are supposed to tell me these things. If I

was Jennifer and I'd told you Brad was making this new film with Angelina, would you have said anything? Like perhaps, 'That's a really bad idea and before you let him go you should restrain him using all available means including tying his testicles to the head of the bed'?"

She's sniggering. "Of course I would."

"And if I was Lisa Marie Presley and I'd told you I was going to marry Michael Jackson because I liked the shape of his nose, or rather, noses, and he's just a sweet boy who loves children, I mean really loves children, and his dramatic change in appearance was undoubtedly a result of a genuine bona fide skin disease, would you have said anything?"

She stops sniggering. "Wait a minute. Are you saying Lisa Marie Presley was married to Michael Jackson in the olden days?"

Cheek. "Don't they teach you kids anything in school these days? Yes. Lisa Marie was married to Michael. Before Nicolas Cage."

"Get out! Nicolas Cage was married to Michael Jackson? Really? Is that legal? That so explains *Ghost Rider.*"

I'm surprised Jill doesn't sue. There was a mix-up at the hospital. There's no way this clever, funny, adorable child is related to Jill, Bethany, Harry and Harry Junior. She is, of course, related to me.

Chapter 17

My body is back.

Weight gain is a common side effect of drugs, and usually considered a minor one. I would suggest that those who consider it minor have not experienced blowing up so big that, when you step on a talking scale it says, "One at a time, please." When there's not just a thin person inside you trying to get out, but several of them. I'm not talking about vanity. I'm talking about your sense of self.

Consider the number of times you see your body. In the mirror and in windows as you walk. Your hands as you type or sort the washing; your legs from the corner of your eye. Showering. Dressing. Putting on your shoes, or rings or makeup. All these times, to be confronted by the sight of someone who is not

you—not-your hands at the end of not-your arms—can fill you with a sense of dislocation each second of each minute of each day.

Once I stopped the medication the weight vanished like I had exfoliated it away with 100 brushes of my extra-scratchy loofah. Without layers of fat insulating me I can feel more, sense more. Now, instead of a small gasp each time I see myself, I feel nothing but a gentle sense of knowing. "Relax," it says. "That leg/arm/hand/tummy is self, not a foreign invader. Stand down."

To tell the truth, the weight didn't vanish entirely of its own accord; I did help. I walk, thousands and thousands of paces. The first Sunday in August, 8 degrees despite winter being almost over, I walk all the way to Chapel Street and north to the river. Then I turn and walk back again. I count the paces in each block and the paces as I cross each street, but I don't write them down. No need to record them. This is not my home. At 12:08 P.M., I see a tall blond man from behind, walking out of the Jam Factory with his arm around a woman's shoulders. When I look closely his hair has not the right curl, his shoulders not the right shape. I think about Nikola until I feel better. Things didn't turn out exactly as he expected either.

By September 1902, Wardenclyffe towered over Long Island at a staggering height of 180 feet. And this was only the building—the iron shell of a tower. There was still no transmitter on top. Nikola planned an enormous copper-plated ball that weighed 55 tons at the top of his tower to conduct radio waves and electricity right across the Atlantic. But he had one small difficulty: he had spent the last of Morgan's money.

I walk down Chapel Street, past shoppers whose only dream is to own more stuff. For Nikola it was never about money or possessions or status. He wrote, pleading, to Morgan, who refused to advance another cent. He became depressed and despairing, and avoided his old friends. Nikola's most important work had come to an end. My work is yet to begin.

Larry comes over almost every day after school. Jill doesn't mind—doesn't press her as to what we do, or ring to check that everything is okay. We sit at my kitchen counter and gossip about the girls at school and rattle on about popular culture and the misogyny of fashion designers and hairdressers. She tells me about the boys she likes and those she doesn't, and bands and TV stars I've never heard of. Occasionally we walk in the park or sprawl on the couch and take turns reading Sherlock Holmes aloud.

One Wednesday afternoon in the middle of August, it's 11 degrees. At 4:13 P.M. we are in my kitchen making raisin cakes dyed purple. Larry's idea.

"Do you have another boyfriend yet?" she says.

"I'm waiting until the line outside my door gets a little longer. Then I'm going to get one of those numbered ticket machines they have at the deli."

"So, you're not going to get back with Seamus?"

"I've moved on. It's a shame Prince Frederik of Denmark is taken."

She leans her elbows on the counter, cradling her chin in her hands. "Dad says you were mad to let Seamus get away. He says you'll never find one like him again."

I drip the purple mix into the cupcake liners. "Yes. Well."

"I liked him."

"If you eat all the mixture we won't have any cake," I say.

"I like the mixture better anyway." She licks the spoon and leaves a purple dollop on her nose.

I love my new job. I should have done this years ago; who would have guessed it was so easy to become a contributing member of society? Monday mornings a uniform-clad courier delivers a new-smelling

cardboard box stuffed with a raft of paper—bills, in-voices, spreadsheets—each in a colored manila folder labeled in a neat hand. Squarish letters in black, flat on the bottom as if they had been written against a ruler. I sit at my desk, in my lumbar-support office chair that I bought over the Internet. I log in to a central mainframe, find the particular job number and type each sheet into the relevant page. In my new morning routine, I start at 8:30 A.M. At exactly 10:30 A.M. or after I finish 50 sheets, whichever is sooner, I go to the coffee shop for coffee and cake, counting my steps as I go. I start work again at 11:15 A.M. Another 50 sheets later, or at 1:15 P.M., I stop for lunch. (No more salad sandwiches because the time it takes to count sprouts is too impractical for my new working-girl life. Now, cheese, ham and tomato on whole wheat. Not whole-grain. All those seeds!) 2 more hours or 50 sheets, then afternoon tea.

Count the hours, count the sheets, then clock off. Most of my invisible colleagues/competitors are either hopelessly unskilled semi-recovering addicts who work from home because it's nearer the scotch, or brain-dead mums with a squawking baby wriggling like a tape-worm off one breast as they type. In a remarkably short period of time, I am the longest-serving employee of the data-entry firm. My fingers fly across the keyboard

like Chopin's and I complete the work in half the time it takes the average typist. Naturally I make no errors.

The salary is poor but it's more than the sickness benefit, which I no longer receive. As well as the meager weekly deposits into my bank account, the company gives generous monthly bonuses designed to motivate the other typing monkeys to go faster. Sometimes they are cash, sometimes movie tickets or restaurant dinners or picnic sets or bottles of wine. I win the bonus every month and keep the cash and prizes. Jill buys the movie tickets and dinners from me, pity clothed as compassion. It seems I will never be rid of this.

Now I have five men in my life. I see more of my Indian boys these days. I know their names (Eshwar, Vandan, Gagan, Mahendra and Murali) but I'm not certain which one's which. I think Vandan is the tall one. Several times a week they bring me sweets— habshi halwa, chewy and nutty; pistachio barfi, delicate like fudge—their mothers have sent from home and samosas they have made themselves. They drop in to see if I need a lightbulb changed or if they can pick up anything for me at the shops. Mahendra and Eshwar (I think) rig both my broadband connection and hard drive to go faster. They ask for nothing but occasional help filling out a government form and once asked me to call a belligerent council employee who had refused

one of them (Gagan?) a parking permit—an experience I found both cathartic and amusing. Had I known that giving away a TV would earn me a helpful Hindu task force I would have done it years ago.

I'm glad I have the Indian boys, because I miss the Germphobics. In some ways they were so right: their rejection of hypocritical greeting handshakes and kisses, their stylish gloves and flowing sleeves. Daria's right; it's not that hard to flush the toilet using your foot. In other ways they were badly wrong: never eating in cafés, never reading a public library book. And, as both my sexual fantasizing and masturbating skills have returned with renewed vigor, refreshed after their little holiday, I wonder how the Germphobics survived without even the thought of sex. I may never hold another man in my arms, but at least I have my imagination.

Nikola stars in my fantasies again. He does. If, while I'm imagining myself as a tight-bodiced serving wench in medieval England, I notice the hair of the tall stranger astride his horse seems lighter than before, I resolutely darken it. And perhaps occasionally the mouth I imagine hot on my inner thigh is framed by sharp, unshaven whiskers instead of a clipped mustache. With some concentration, Nikola's features remain fine and sculptured. But sometimes my visions need a firm hand.

Francine I don't miss, because somehow she is still with me. I think of her when I see flowers or count rubber bands or hear a New Age guru on the radio. I wonder what will become of her; with her sweet, Swiss-cheese brain I fear the influence of years of Germphobics will pull her under. She'll be sitting on the other side of the circle, scrubbing hands and chairs, in no time.

Sunday night. 8:30. 12 degrees. Larry is on the phone.

"So," she says.

"So, what?"

"Do you have another boyfriend yet?"

"Larry. Are you opening a dating service?"

"I'm not nagging. But I'm in the school play next month. And it would be great if you could come."

It would. I remember her violin recital. Holding hands. "The trouble is, no one can compare with Nikola."

"Are you still banging on about him?"

I curl my feet up on the couch. From here I can see his picture beside the bed. I could swear he was smiling.

"Me? Never."

"Grace, he went broke. You told me yourself."

"Well."

"And that stupid tower? It never worked, did it?"

I stretch out on the couch, moving aside the book I'd been reading. "Not worked as such. During World War I the government blew it up. They thought German spies would use it to track American shipping. It was sold as scrap metal. For $1,750."

"See? And what happened to Nikola?"

"Well . . . not a lot. He lived the rest of his life alone in a hotel room, broke. He started releasing kooky statements about communicating with other planets, and told everyone he invented a death ray gun."

"That's the only cool part of the story, a death ray gun. The rest is a downer."

"It isn't a downer, Larry. This is a terrific story of the power and the burden of someone who thinks differently from the rest of us."

"Doesn't sound like it to me."

I try to think of a better way to say this. It's important she understands.

"Look, it's easy to think that, if only Nikola had been more realistic and practical, his story would not have ended this way. He would have been wealthy beyond his dreams, and his fortune would have financed more research. If Nikola Tesla had been wealthy, the world today would be unrecognizable to us."

"That's what I think. If he was so smart why couldn't he get it together?"

"An awful lot of smart people don't have it together. The fact is this: if he had been more realistic and practical, odds are he would have stayed at home on the farm in Serbia and become a priest like his father wanted him to. He would have married a hardworking, practical farm girl, and raised sturdy, practical children."

He would not have been the most famous man in the world for a time, or been honored with a Yugoslav stamp and banknote bearing his face. He would never have invented radio—a claim vindicated by the U.S. Supreme Court in 1943 when it ruled that Marconi's patent was a deliberate copy of Nikola's. He would not be remembered with a statue at Niagara Falls, where his genius allowed electricity to be captured, and the unit of magnetic flux density would not be known as the tesla.

"But he died like one of those crazy recluses, like Leonardo DiCaprio in that movie. Howard Hughes. He . . . Look, sorry, Grace, but he was a bit of a loser, wasn't he. 'Cause he was so nutty."

He's still smiling at me from beside the bed. He's okay with this. He was never ashamed of how he was. Nikola died of a coronary thrombosis on January 7, 1943, alone in his bed at the Hotel New Yorker. Suite

3327. He was 86 years old and so obsessed with a fear of germs that he received few visitors. But his eulogy was read live over the radio by the mayor of New York and thousands of people came to his funeral. Serbs sat on one side of the cathedral and Croats on the other, all there to bid farewell to the greatest of their countrymen.

"Larry, Nikola was not a loser. He was different. That's what made him special. It was his gift. Unlike those average people, he will never be forgotten."

"What do you mean by 'average'? We're doing that in math."

I don't know. Medium looks, works at the box office, likes football and barbecues. Lives in Carnegie. "You know. Average. Normal."

"Average doesn't mean normal."

I sit up so quickly that *Guyton's Textbook of Medical Physiology* clatters to the floor. "What?"

"Average doesn't mean normal. The average means you divide the total of something by the number of things in it. So the average can actually be unique."

I can feel a vein throbbing in the side of my face where I'm resting the phone. Of course. She's right. " 'The average can actually be unique.' "

"I just said that. I've got an exam on this tomorrow. Do you mean the median, which is the thing that's in the middle? Or the mode, which means the most common thing?"

All this time. It wasn't only that he was taller. It was all the little things, like the way he made me laugh and how his eyelashes fluttered when he slept. How he put up with living with his brothers. The way he tasted. The way time would slow down when I was waiting for him to come over. How he was always so proud of me.

"Grace? Are you there?" I can hear a wobbly elation; all these years of being told things by adults, of asking questions, of listening, and now she has taught me something. Something important. Yet I don't know whether to be grateful.

The next Saturday morning, 9:15 A.M. 15 degrees. I walk home from my new supermarket with plastic shopping bags slicing my fingers. This is the worst of my shopping days, a day that comes rarely but I still dread it. Laundry powder. 10 boxes of laundry powder, 5 in each bag, as well as my food for the week. Every 100 paces I stop and release my fingers so the blood can return to the red strangled flesh.

I am walking High Street when I see him. Seamus. He's standing at a tram stop on the other side of the road.

For a moment I stare as though he was an actor from a medical drama I used to watch on TV: familiar, but so out of context that I couldn't place him without his lab coat. For another second I don't believe it's him,

I'm that used to seeing his doppelgangers wherever I look. Now his face jolts me and my heart thuds. He is wearing a navy polo shirt and those pale denim jeans with the faded knees. Boat shoes fresh out of *21 Jump Street*. Someone should tell him it's no longer 1988. Perhaps I should, but my legs barely move. I lean against a fence.

At first he does not see me. Perhaps I fall outside his field of vision or he's concentrating on something else. But the human mind has a talent for ignoring what is inconvenient for it to notice. A built-in delete key to soften the blows of regret or guilt.

Or, and this is more likely, he doesn't see me because I look fabulous. Had I still been fat, frumpy and half asleep, he would have spotted me straightaway.

His tram comes and he climbs on, solicitously allowing an old lady in front of him. Through the windows I watch him find a seat. It isn't until the tram begins moving that he sees me. He stares and his mouth opens wider. Then he holds up one palm against the window, fingers spread. The tram rattles away.

I lean against the wall, head in my hands. It takes a few minutes before I can pick up the groceries again.

Exactly a week later, 27th of August, it's my 36th birthday. Jill hosts a family dinner. Somehow I manage to attend. In the morning I walk to Glenferrie Road

and buy a party dress: a dark green jersey wrap with long sleeves. This is now my official Winter Function Dress, to be worn during the months of June, July and August to all events that are outside of my normal routine. Not that there's a lot of these. I'm glad I bought it too; everyone dresses up. Even Harry strives to reflect his personality. He wears a suit.

Jill throws together a simple meal of pâté de campagne with cornichons, saffron seafood pot-au-feu and passion-fruit crème brulées with poached quince. My single crème brulée has a single sparkler sticking out of the top. Jill must believe I would find a cake with 36 candles depressing. I bring a bottle of wine I found in the wooden bin in the front of the liquor store on Burke Road. When I give it to Harry, he grimaces and tries to hide it down the back of the wine rack without my noticing. Jill gives me a jar of vanilla-scented bath salts wrapped in soft pink tissue paper from her and Harry and Bethany. It has escaped her that a) my flat has no bath, b) even if it did, in these times of water rationing it would be immoral to take one, and c) I would be the last person on earth who would want to smell like vanilla. What does she think I am? A crème brûlée?

Larry, glorious, wonderful Larry, gives me a new biography of Nikola she ordered on the 'net. Perhaps she is a little sorry that she judged him so harshly last time we spoke. Harry Junior gives me a gorgeous

clutch purse in reds and golds made from an antique kimono material. He is proud of his choice, pointing out the detail in the fabric and the design of the clasp while his father squirms. I am so delighted I whisper later that if ever he feels like sewing he can come over to my flat and no one need ever know. I have been meaning to buy a sewing machine anyway—anything to avoid visiting shopping centers. He hugs himself with excitement.

Mother gives me a magnificent purple flowering orchid she grew herself. A greater gift from Mother is the gratitude she shows to Jill as we leave, hugging her and thanking her for the lovely dinner, and who would have guessed meatloaf, fish soup and blancmange could go together so well. Jill drives me home, her cheery face unusually glum.

It is 10 past 10 (allowable birthday variation to routine) when she drops me off. As I walk along the top-floor balcony I almost miss it. In the shadows, propped up against my door is a small box around 10.5 centimeters square and 3 centimeters high, wrapped in orange/tan paper with an orange/tan ribbon. No card. I put down my plastic bag of gifts and the orchid, and pick up the box. I feel the weight of it, the shape of it. It has been a long time since I have held something like this, but I remember. I know what this is.

I unpeel the tape a piece at a time, one from each end and one from the middle, unwrapping it without tearing so I can keep even the paper. At last the box lies heavy in my hand. The dark green plastic box. I open the lid to make sure they're all there. The top layer is full, and when I put my hand flat they slide around a little. My fingers trace the embossing: NUMBER-RODS-IN-COLOR (FOR CUISENAIRE MATHEMATICS). It is a complete set of vintage rods, identical to the ones I threw away. I can see myself sitting on my bed and playing with them like I used to—tossing them and listening to the almost-metallic tinkling of their midair collisions. Waking in the morning to the sight of colored rods scattered across the quilt, some still clasped in my hands. It's only now, holding them like this, that I realize how much I've missed them. A secondhand child's game. My eyes fill with tears.

There's no one on the landing. I peer over the railing. From here I can look down to the atrium. There are some struggling trees and 12 mismatched potted plants belonging to flat 2. There is a figure down below, looking up at me.

For a moment I stare at him.

"Seamus Joseph O'Reilly. Hi."

Chapter 18

"Grace Lisa Vandenburg. Happy 36th birth-day."

I'd like to grip the railing but I can't let go of the box. "And I don't look a day over 35, right?"

"Fishing for compliments? I can't see your face from way down here. To tell you how wonderful you look I'd have to come up."

No. Go away. I told you to piss off 15 weeks, 6 days and 16 and a half hours ago.

"Or I could stay here," he says, "and we could do the balcony scene from *Romeo and Juliet*."

Any moment now one of the Indian boys will hear us and stick his head out to see that I'm okay. "I think you know the way."

I watch him take every step. 44. He arrives on the landing. He takes 7 steps toward me.

"You're a hard woman to catch. I came around a few times. And I've called." He reaches out and holds the railing with his right hand.

He's wearing brown boots, his pale jeans and a green check shirt. Brown leather jacket unzipped, hands deep in the pockets. Perhaps he's on his way to a rodeo. His hair is a little shorter than I remember. I wonder if it feels different. I wonder how long he's been standing down there.

"Only 23 times," I say. "Quitter."

The air is cold and because I was only walking from the car I haven't put on my jacket. With my spare hand I rub my arm.

"I hope they're right," he says. "I tried to remember. I wanted them to be exactly the same. Yours were a collector's item."

I hold the rods under the light outside my door. The green box glistens. "They're perfect. How did you possibly find them?"

"On eBay. It's amazing the things people hold on to."

Some child, somewhere, learned to count with these. Perhaps many children. Tiny hands, making pyramids and lines and stacks. "Thank you, Seamus. It was very thoughtful of you."

He brings one hand to his face and rubs his chin. "So, to clarify. You're grateful?"

"I beg your pardon?"

"I said, are you grateful? For the rods?"

I don't recall anyone ever asking me that before. It takes a while to find a response. "Um, I suppose, yes. I'm not giving away my firstborn child or anything, but yes, I suppose I am grateful."

"So, you know what gratitude feels like?"

"Um, yes. My parents fed and clothed me. Sent me to school. I'm 36 now; that's a lot of birthday presents. I've actually been grateful before."

He nods. "And I know you know what guilt feels like."

This is stupid. I'm cold. I could just say good night. I could say, thanks for the gift, Seamus, and go inside and stop this inane conversation. It would be so easy. I'm only 5 paces from my door. Walk, and put the key in the lock. Turn it. Open the door, go inside. But his lovely eyes have an intensity I've not seen in them before.

I turn my head to the side and look over the railing again. "Yes, Seamus. Yes, I know what guilt feels like."

"And you know what it feels like to try to be someone you're not."

I put the rods in my bag of presents and fold my arms. "Yep. Lots of experience at that. Considering doing my Ph.D. in trying to be someone you're not."

He takes 2 steps toward me. He holds on to my arms. I can feel his hands warm through the fabric of my dress.

"So, we've established that you know what gratitude, guilt and pretending feel like."

He's so close to me now. At first all I can do is nod.

"What do you want, Seamus?" My voice is too low.

"I don't want any confusion about what happens from here."

Those beautiful eyes. "What . . . what happens from here, Seamus?"

Slowly he lowers his head and he kisses me. A soft kiss. I had forgotten how this meeting of lips liquefies my bones. It's been centuries since I've been kissed by him. I close my eyes.

"I . . . I need to tell you . . ."

"Hmm?"

"I . . . therapy . . . I dropped out. Stopped the medication. The counseling. Everything."

"Honesty. Good start. I know, Grace. I spoke with Francine. She said something about carnations. Don't change the subject."

"What was the subject again?"

"Was there any gratitude, guilt or pretending in that kiss?"

I realize I'm gripping his shirt, my fingers threaded through between the buttons to touch the skin of his chest.

"I'm not 100 percent sure. Can you do it again?"

This time my hands leave his shirt and twirl around his neck. I remember the feel of his hair, the way the curls go in different directions. I remember the feeling of my breasts pressing against his chest. I remember everything. When he stops kissing me, my lips chase his. I open my eyes.

"Well?" He's frowning, staring.

"Let me see. Nope. No gratitude. No guilt. No pretending."

"No more lies, Grace."

"It wasn't a lie. It wasn't meant to be a lie, but I can't talk about it. I can't think about it. I can't even remember what I was doing, you know? That's the worst part. The thing I was doing that was so important that I didn't close the door—I don't even know what that was."

"It's okay, Grace. It's okay."

"It's almost his birthday. We'd be planning a party for next month. He could have been a builder or a sailor or a chef. He might have loved skiing or cycling. Everything would have been different."

He holds me for a long time without speaking. "Everything is not so bad," he says. "A lot of it was my

fault. I'm sorry, Grace. Truly, it wasn't about changing you or rescuing you. I just wanted you to be happy."

He's warm. I can feel his heart beating. "Everything is fine," I say.

He reaches behind his neck and unwraps my arms. Returns them to my sides and strokes them. "Good. Great. Well, good night, Grace."

Before I know it he's at the top of the stairs.

"What? Just where do you think you're going?"

He turns. A cheeky grin. "I'm going home now. Good night."

I stomp toward him, maybe 5 or 6 steps. I lose count. "Listen to me, banana boy. You can't just kiss me like that and then say good night."

He grins and puts his hands on my shoulders. "I think part of the problem last time was that we started off a bit fast. I think it scared you. The fact is, I went out with you because I liked you. You, Grace, just as you were. Not you as raw material for the new improved Grace. I know the therapy was my idea, but . . . God, I can't be brilliant all the time. This time we're going to take it easy, really get to know each other. No rush. In a week or so I'll ring you. And then we'll have coffee. Then in a few months we'll hold hands. No rush."

If I still had the rods in my hand I would have smacked him over the head with them.

"That must be the single most stupid idea I've ever heard in my life. At least it's in the top 10. Do you think we'll live to be a hundred? Or have you decided to become a Buddhist and pray we have plenty of time together in your next life?"

He laughs. "I'm just trying to do the right thing."

"The right thing, huh? So in a week or so, you'll ring me." His shirt is tucked into his jeans. I yank it out. He doesn't move.

"Yes."

"And then maybe we'll have coffee." His shirt has 6 buttons, pearl-colored plastic. I undo the bottom one.

"That's what I said. Yes."

"Then we work our way up to holding hands? In a few months, if we feel like we're ready." I undo another button. My fingers brush the warm skin of his stomach.

He gulps. "No rush."

"And . . ." Button 3. "After that?" Button 4. "After we hold hands?" Button 5.

"Grace . . . Grace, it's freezing."

"I can fix that." Button 6. "Come inside."

Chapter 19

It's not perfect. Problems still pop up sometimes, but it's surprising how things can be managed with a bit of imagination. Of the many things that have changed about my life, the most remarkable must be football. I love it. Seamus was right, that first morning we woke up together last summer. It is glorious. It's all about numbers: touches, handballs, kicks, marks, percentage. And each player has a number on his back! How long has this been going on? Saturday afternoon has become the highlight of my week, although we also go on a Sunday if Hawthorn is playing. We need to arrive a little early so I can have my ham, cheese and tomato on whole wheat, brought from home, at exactly 1:15 P.M. Seamus has a revolting meat pie and a beer any time he wants. Seamus misses all the good counting bits, but

he seems content to sit with his arm around my shoulders and watch the game. Cricket season is coming up. Seamus says I'll like that even more once I get my head around strike rates, batting averages and run-rate per over. I believe him.

Larry and Jill and Mother are delighted I am back with Seamus. We go to see Larry in the school play (she is Levi in a horrible performance of *Joseph and the Amazing Technicolor Dreamcoat*). Mother especially adores him (Seamus, not Andrew Lloyd Webber). He is full of anecdotes of wonderful football injuries, like knees smashing cheekbones and eye sockets, and shins shoving noses through the front of skulls. My mother has never been a sports fan before; now, with Seamus's guidance, she never misses a game on TV. Shoulder reconstructions, anterior cruciates. She's becoming an expert. Next year, Marjorie, he tells her, I'll take you to the motor racing. She can hardly wait.

One memorable day during the school holidays I take some time off work and Larry and I catch the bus to Chadstone. We sit in the food court. Larry chooses where we sit, then leaves to stand in line for a burger and chips. When she comes back to the table, she holds my hand, and when she notices my eyes shut or my breathing become shallow, she speaks soft words in my

ear about courage and triumph and how proud she is of her aunt. Her favorite aunt.

We don't manage to stay long (the array of chairs, uncountable because of people sitting, standing and moving, is unsettling and I have an allergy to something—I begin to itch uncontrollably) but she doesn't seem to mind and helps me outside, again with her arm in mine. As soon as we are in the fresh air the itching stops, so perhaps it was caused by toxic gas coming off the plastic. It may have been fleas but they would have hung about for longer, I'm sure. We take a taxi back to my café where I buy her a chocolate muffin and a Diet Coke.

And all this time I never lecture her. I give her no advice, tell her no analogies or homilies. I compare her with no one. Because there are some things you must find out for yourself. But if there was just one thing that I could give to this beautiful child—just one thing I could hand her, wrapped in shiny paper and finished with a stiff bow, this is what I would tell her.

Most people miss their whole lives, you know. Listen, life isn't when you are standing on top of a mountain looking at the sunset. Life isn't waiting at the altar or the moment your child is born or that time you were swimming in deep water and a dolphin came up alongside you. These are fragments. 10 or 12 grains of

sand spread throughout your entire existence. These are not life. Life is brushing your teeth or making a sandwich or watching the news or waiting for the bus. Or walking. Every day, thousands of tiny events happen and if you're not watching, if you're not careful, if you don't capture them and make them count, you could miss it.

You could miss your whole life.

Acknowledgments

For information about the life of Nikola Tesla, I am indebted to Margaret Cheney's *Tesla: Man Out of Time*, and to Marc J. Seifer for *Wizard: The Life and Times of Nikola Tesla*. Any errors remain my own (or Grace's).

I owe much to the wonderful Clifford A. Pickover's *Wonders of Numbers: Adventures in Mathematics, Mind and Meaning*, which was filled with fascinating information about numbers. And I am grateful to www.crimelibrary.com for facts on the trial and death of William Kemmler.

My thanks must also go to those readers who gave me helpful advice, especially Keren Barnett, Melissa Cranenburgh, Jess Howard, Irene Korsten, Caroline Lee, Fiona Mackrell, Jess Obersby, Steve Wide and

Chris Womersley. Friends were generous with their ideas and support, in particular Lee Falvey, Scott Falvey and Lee Miller.

Special thanks go to Peter Bishop and the supporters of Varuna writers' retreat, where I wrote part of this novel, and to RMIT's Professional Writing and Editing faculty, particularly Olga Lorenzo. I am incredibly grateful to Michael Williams for believing this manuscript could count, and to the brilliant and inspiring book lovers at Text Publishing, especially Michael Heyward.